THY

AUSTRALIAN AMATEUR ...)K 4

MORGANA BEST

The Prawn Identity
Australian Amateur Sleuth, Book 4
Copyright © 2016 by Morgana Best
All Rights Reserved
ISBN 9781925674248

No part of this book may be reproduced in any form or by any electronic or mechanical means, including information storage and retrieval systems, without written permission from the author, except for the use of brief quotations in a book review.

This is a work of fiction. Any resemblance to any person, living or dead, is purely coincidental. The personal names have been invented by the author, and any likeness to the name of any person, living or dead, is purely coincidental.

This book might contain references to specific commercial products, process or service by trade name, trademark, manufacturer, or otherwise, specific brand-name products and/or trade names of products, which are trademarks or registered trademarks and/or trade names, and these are property of their respective owners. Morgana Best or her associates have no association with any specific commercial products, process, or service by trade name, trademark, manufacturer, or otherwise, specific brand-name products and / or trade names of products.

GLOSSARY

Some Australian spellings and expressions are entirely different from US spellings and expressions. Below are just a few examples. It would take an entire book to list all the differences.

The author has used Australian spelling in this series. Here are a few examples: *Mum* instead of the US spelling *Mom*, *neighbour* instead of the US spelling *neighbor*, *realise* instead of the US spelling *realize*. It is *Ms*, *Mr* and *Mrs* in Australia, not *Ms.*, *Mr.* and *Mrs.*; *defence* not *defense*; *judgement* not *judgment*; *cosy* and not *cozy*; *1930s* not *1930's*; *offence* not *offense*; *centre* not *center*; *towards* not *toward*; *jewellery* not *jewelry*; *favour* not *favor*; *mould* not *mold*; *two storey house* not *two story house*; *practise* (verb) not *practice* (verb); *odour* not *odor*; *smelt* not *smelled*; *travelling* not *traveling*; *liquorice* not *licorice*; *cheque* not *check*; *leant* not *leaned*; *have concussion* not *have a concussion*; *anti clockwise* not *counterclockwise*; *go to hospital* not *go to the hospital*; *sceptic* not *skeptic*; *aluminium* not *aluminum*; *learnt* not *learned*. We have *fancy dress* parties not *costume* parties. We don't say *gotten*. We say *car crash* (or *accident*) not *car wreck*. We say *a herb* not *an herb* as we produce the 'h.'

We might say (a company name) *are* instead of *is*.

The above are just a few examples.

It's not only different words; Aussies sometimes use different expressions in sentence structure. We might *eat a curry* not *eat curry*. We might say *in the main street* not *on the main street*. Someone might be *going well* instead of *doing well*. We might say *without drawing breath* not *without drawing a breath*.

These are just some of the differences.

Please note that these are not mistakes or typos, but correct, normal Aussie spelling, terms, and syntax.

AUSTRALIAN SLANG AND TERMS

Benchtops - counter tops (kitchen)

Big Smoke - a city

Blighter - infuriating or good-for-nothing person

Blimey! - an expression of surprise

Bloke - a man (usually used in nice sense, "a good bloke")

Blue (noun) - an argument ("to have a blue")

Bluestone - copper sulphate (copper sulfate in US spelling)

Bluo - a blue laundry additive, an optical brightener

Boot (car) - trunk (car)

Bonnet (car) - hood (car)

Bore - a drilled water well

Budgie smugglers (variant: budgy smugglers) - named after the Aussie native bird, the budgerigar. A slang term for brief and tight-fitting men's swimwear

Bugger! - as an expression of surprise, not a swear word

Bugger - as in "the poor bugger" - refers to an unfortunate person (not a swear word)

Bunging it on - faking something, pretending

Bush telegraph - the grapevine, the way news spreads by word of mouth in the country

Car park - parking lot

Cark it - die
Chooks - chickens
Come good - turn out okay
Copper, cop - police officer
Coot - silly or annoying person
Cream bun - a sweet bread roll with copious amounts of cream, plus jam in the centre
Crook - 1. "Go crook (on someone)" - to berate them. 2. (someone is) crook - (someone is) ill. 3. Crook (noun) - a criminal
Demister (in car) - defroster
Drongo - an idiot
Dunny - an outhouse, an outdoor toilet building, often ramshackle
Fair crack of the whip - a request to be fair, reasonable, just
Flannelette (fabric) - cotton, wool, or synthetic fabric, one side of which has a soft finish.
Flat out like a lizard drinking water - very busy
Galah - an idiot
Garbage - trash
G'day - Hello
Give a lift (to someone) - give a ride (to someone)
Goosebumps - goose pimples
Gumboots - rubber boots, wellingtons
Knickers - women's underwear

Laundry (referring to the room) - laundry room
Lamingtons - iconic Aussie cakes, square, sponge, chocolate-dipped, and coated with desiccated coconut. Some have a layer of cream and strawberry jam (= jelly in US) between the two halves.
Lift - elevator
Like a stunned mullet - very surprised
Mad as a cut snake - either insane or very angry
Mallee bull (as fit as, as mad as) - angry and/or fit, robust, super strong.
Miles - while Australians have kilometres these days, it is common to use expressions such as, "The road stretched for miles," "It was miles away."
Moleskins - woven heavy cotton fabric with suede-like finish, commonly used as working wear, or as town clothes
Mow (grass / lawn) - cut (grass / lawn)
Neenish tarts - Aussie tart. Pastry base. Filling is based on sweetened condensed milk mixture or mock cream. Some have layer of raspberry jam (jam = jelly in US). Topping is in two equal halves: icing (= frosting in US), usually chocolate on one side, and either lemon or pink on the other.
Pub - The pub at the south of a small town is

often referred to as the 'bottom pub' and the pub at the north end of town, the 'top pub.' The size of a small town is often judged by the number of pubs - i.e. "It's a three pub town."

Red cattle dog - (variant: blue cattle dog usually known as a 'blue dog') - referring to the breed of Australian Cattle Dog. However, a 'red dog' is usually a red kelpie (another breed of dog)

Shoot through - leave

Shout (a drink) - to buy a drink for someone

Skull (a drink) - drink a whole drink without stopping

Stone the crows! - an expression of surprise

Takeaway (food) - Take Out (food)

Toilet - also refers to the room if it is separate from the bathroom

Torch - flashlight

Tuck in (to food) - to eat food hungrily

Ute / Utility - pickup truck

Vegemite - Australian food spread, thick, dark brown

Wardrobe - closet

Windscreen - windshield

Indigenous References

Bush tucker - food that occurs in the Australian bush

Koori - the original inhabitants/traditional custodians of the land of Australia in the part of NSW in which this book is set. *Murri* are the people just to the north. White European culture often uses the term, *Aboriginal people*.

CHAPTER 1

"No, you can't come back in," I said, determined to stand my ground. "You'll just eat everything. I'll let you back in when they've gone."

Sandy looked up at me, giving me her absolute best puppy eyes. She was making it quite clear that staying outside wasn't her first choice.

"It's not even raining out, so you'll be fine!" I sighed. "I'll go get you a treat. Stay there," I said, hoping to appease Sandy until my friends had left. She was a good dog, if a little too friendly around people, but she was also very excitable, and... a Labrador. If I let her in, she'd try to eat absolutely *anything* that they brought. Possibly even the guests themselves, if I didn't keep an eye on her.

I came back with her treat and was greeted with an excited little dance. Not to sound like I was profiling her, but Sandy was a typical Labrador in every imaginable way, including—but not limited to—complete obedience so long as she was brought food. I threw the treat out into the yard and closed the door, knowing she'd entertain herself until I could bring her back inside.

Right on cue, the doorbell rang. I rushed to open it and was greeted with a huge platter of sandwiches.

"Here you go, Sibyl," Mr Buttons said as he handed them to me, smiling warmly. "I know you're making lunch, but I thought it was best that I contribute."

I looked at the platter. Sure enough, the sandwiches were missing their crusts. I noticed bits of green sticking out from the bread and immediately knew that they were cucumber sandwiches with the crusts cut off. I'd call them Mr Button's specialty, but I was unsure if he really made anything else, other than tea, of course. Mr Buttons was the only permanent boarder at Cressida's boarding house, and he was best described as a typical butler. He was an older English man with a penchant for dressing well and cleanliness. Actually, *penchant* doesn't cover it. He was a neat freak, plain and simple. I was almost worried about how obsessive he was with ensuring that everything was clean. It was especially bad when I invited him over to my own house as I had today, which always meant spending the previous day cleaning furiously so as not to upset him.

"Thank you, Mr Buttons," I said cheerily. "I always look forward to these sandwiches."

"I've done something a bit different this time," Mr Buttons said with a shy smile. "I do hope it's not too drastic."

"Hello, Sibyl!" Cressida stepped out from behind Mr Buttons and hugged me warmly. I nimbly moved the platter out of the way to avoid squashing it and hugged her back. Cressida was, in a word, eccentric. She was the owner of the boarding house, sporting bright red curly hair and entirely too much makeup. She also spoke to her cat, Lord Farringdon, which isn't as strange as the fact that she thought he spoke back to her.

"I've brought you a present." Cressida handed me a large platter with a cover. I thanked her, set the sandwich platter down and took the cover off, revealing a tiny canvas. I felt the colour flush to my face as I immediately recognised what it was. A painting. Cressida's work was always unsettling, to say the very least. She was one of the kindest and nicest people I'd ever met, in spite of her hobby of painting incredibly gory and unsettling images. I swallowed hard and flipped the canvas over to see what it was, fighting back the onset of nausea. It was, as expected, one of the hardest things to look at that I could imagine.

"It's, uh, beautiful. Thank you, Cressida." I tried my best to smile. "I really like the, um... the colours you've used."

"Oh, I'm glad you noticed." Cressida beamed. "I used a yellow chiffon colour for the bits of fat, complemented by rosewood and rust for the blood." She smiled as she spoke, though I spent more of my time trying not to pass out than I did listening. "I also made it small so you can hang it for your guests!"

Well, it would deter burglars, I thought grimly. *And everybody else.* "Come in. Make yourselves comfortable," I said, beckoning them inside and closing the door. "I've made a lemon roast chicken with vegetables. Nothing too fancy, but I hope you enjoy it!"

"Well, it smells delicious," Cressida said earnestly as Mr Buttons busied himself by dusting off my table. I sighed, but knew no matter how much I'd cleaned he would have done something like this anyway. I wasn't even sure if he could help himself.

I dished up the sandwiches Mr Buttons had brought while Sandy watched hungrily from outside, trying her best to look cute in order to get some leftovers. I did my best to ignore her and served the sandwiches to my guests, and then we sat around and talked. Lunch proper was still a while away, so I thought it would be a good way to pass some time. I bit into the cucumber sandwich and recoiled, dropping it on the table.

"What was that?" I asked, realising that I might have offended Mr Buttons.

"Oh, like I mentioned, I decided to try something different. Instead of cucumber, I used watercress and coriander, but felt it was somewhat flavourless, so I put some garlic ketchup on them as well," Mr Buttons explained, as though it was the most normal thought process in the world.

"It's, uh, great. Thank you. But to be candid, I think I preferred the cucumber," I admitted, hoping not to hurt his feelings. Mr Buttons smiled and nodded, apparently agreeing. Cressida seemed to be avoiding the sandwiches altogether. For a woman who spent most of her free time having conversations with her cat, she was showing a remarkable level of wisdom.

Cressida walked over to a window. "We need rain so desperately. The grass crackles under your feet when you walk on it."

"Winter is coming," Mr Buttons said.

I chuckled. "Have you been watching Game of Thrones?"

Mr Buttons looked startled. "Whatever do you mean, Sibyl?"

I shrugged. "Never mind."

"I'll check the weather app on my iPhone," Cressida announced proudly. "That will tell us if it's raining."

"You can see for yourself that it's not raining, Cressida," Mr Buttons said patiently. He shot me a look. Mr Buttons had recently, and with some difficulty, talked Cressida into getting a smart phone, and I was surprised when he had succeeded, because Cressida was technologically challenged. However, Cressida had taken to the smart phone like a duck to water.

"But my weather app says there is ninety

percent chance of rain in ten minutes," she insisted, tapping her phone.

Mr Buttons sighed. "It's clearly not raining, is it? There's not a cloud in the sky."

As Cressida continued to insist that it would rain in ten minutes, I excused myself to get lunch. The chicken had turned out perfectly, with the skin being browned but not burnt, and the lemon having infused the meat nicely. I dished it up to the happy pair.

"This is delicious, Sibyl!" Mr Buttons exclaimed between mouthfuls. "Much better than anything that Dorothy could cook, the daft cow." He seethed. Cressida and I exchanged shocked glances. Dorothy was the newest cook at the boarding house, though she wasn't all that new any more. It was no surprise that she didn't get along with Mr Buttons or, well, anybody. Despite that, it was more than a small shock to hear Mr Buttons say something so blunt.

Dorothy spent less of her time cooking and more of her time complaining and being rude. On top of all that, she wasn't even great at cooking, consistently providing average or flavourless meals. I suspected Cressida didn't fire her simply because she was scared of what would happen if she did.

"You can't say something like that, Mr Buttons," Cressida said in the sternest tone she could muster.

"Quite right, quite right," Mr Buttons said with a sigh. "I apologise. She just irks me more than anybody I've met," he admitted.

"I understand, but maybe she'll come around if we're kind to her," I suggested, not entirely convincing even myself. My suggestion was greeted with even less convinced stares, so I resigned myself to just eating my lunch and avoiding the topic entirely.

"I'm sorry to keep bringing it up, but why haven't you fired her, Cressida? She can't cook this well. Maybe Sibyl could be our new cook!" Mr Buttons proposed quite excitedly.

I narrowly avoided choking on a bit of chicken and cleared my throat. "I'm not sure that's entirely where I want my career path to go, Mr Buttons," I admitted. It's not that I had anything against the idea of being a cook per se, but that I didn't enjoy cooking enough to want to pursue it as a career. As a matter of fact, it was something I actively avoided unless I was cooking for guests.

"Oh, I don't want to upset poor Dorothy," Cressida said sadly. "She can be a handful, but I don't want to hurt her feelings." She continued to pick at her food. I considered that maybe Cressida should just hang some of her paintings in the kitchen as a sure-fire way to make Dorothy quit, but I realised it would also stop any new boarders.

"Well, that's quite good of you, Cressida," Mr Buttons said stoutly. "But I think Dorothy is a..."

"Stupid cow!" a voice screeched loudly. Cressida's jaw fell open as she looked at Mr Buttons, who seemed to be equally shocked. My cockatoo, Max, had flown in from an open window and started screeching and swearing, as usual. At one point my ex husband had found it funny to teach Max to say all sorts of awful things. Unfortunately, it seemed impossible to get Max to learn anything else, or at least forget his insults.

"Max!" I yelled, jumping up and trying to grab him. He fluttered about calling me all sorts of things best left unsaid until I finally got a hold of him and took him into another room. I sat him on his perch and gave him a treat, which he ate happily while calling me every four-letter word I could think of. Well, I could only think of one, but Max could think of more. And then there were the adjectives.

I walked back to the table and apologised after I washed my hands and sat down.

"That's quite all right, Sibyl," Mr Buttons said. "We're used to Max and his antics, or as used to them as one could possibly be. Have you considered taking him to a trainer?"

"Well, sort of," I explained. "There's not exactly an abundance of cockatoo trainers in a small country town like this, but I did find two in Tamworth. Both times I took him there he swore at them so severely they turned me down," I admitted, sighing.

"Surely they'd be used to things like that?" Cressida asked.

"I don't think anybody's used to the things he was saying, Cressida. I won't repeat them, but it's safe to say that I don't exactly blame the trainers for turning me down. I don't have too many guests anyway, so I'm not all that worried about it, except for incidents like just now," I said with a small laugh.

Mr Buttons nodded and spoke to Cressida. "Speaking of guests, has the boarding house been picking up in business since all the nastiness stopped?"

"Nastiness?" Cressida asked with one eyebrow raised. "Oh! You mean the murders." Mr Buttons and I exchanged uncomfortable glances. "Yes, it has a little. I don't suspect that will keep up," she said sadly.

"Why not?" I asked. "It's statistically impossible that we'll have another murder here. I know I've said this sort of thing before, but I really think our town, or at least your boarding house, is all murdered out, so to speak." We'd had more than our fair share of tragedy, but it truly seemed impossible that another murder could occur at the boarding house unless it was haunted or something.

"Well, I wouldn't be so sure," Cressida said. "I've heard that there is indeed another murder coming."

Mr Buttons and I looked at Cressida wide-eyed. "Whatever do you mean?" Mr Buttons asked, shocked. "Who said that?"

"Why, Lord Farringdon, of course," Cressida said simply.

I sighed out loud with a mixture of relief and dismay. On the one hand I was upset that Cressida was still taking her cat's advice seriously, but on the other hand I was relieved that there wasn't really anything wrong.

"I have to disagree with Lord Farringdon this time, Cressida," I said with a smile. "There won't be another murder at the boarding house. It's just impossible."

CHAPTER 2

"How are you with prawns?" Cressida asked, as soon as I answered my phone.

"Prawns?" I was bewildered.

"I need your help."

"I just woke up." I sat up in bed and rubbed my eyes. I'd had a long day of dog grooming clients the previous day and had been up late grooming toy poodles for an important dog show.

"Dorothy had a run-in with Lisa, the new boarder, last night."

I groaned. "Let me guess. Lisa said something about her cooking?" I could feel a headache coming on. Dorothy had never read *How to Win Friends and Influence People*.

"Yes," Cressida's voice boomed, "and I need to have a nice breakfast for Lisa Summers and her husband, Greg, what with them being honeymooners and all. Oh, don't worry, Mr Buttons is here now. He can help me with breakfast." And with that, she hung up.

I snuggled back down into my blankets, and drifted off for what seemed like only seconds, before I was jerked from sleep once more.

I reached out and knocked my phone to the floor, thankful that it didn't fall on Sandy, who was sleeping in her usual spot next to my bed, snoring loudly. I snatched up the phone, slid my thumb across the screen and held it to my ear. "Hello?" I put on my best no-I-didn't-just-wake-up voice.

"Get up here fast," Cressida said in a hushed voice.

"Mr Buttons made a mess of the breakfast?" I guessed.

I wasn't sure what Cressida said next, as every atom in my body froze in shock, but I did catch the words, *death*, and *back yard*.

I was at once wide awake, the words Cressida had spoken causing adrenaline to course through my system. I jumped out of bed and pulled on my jeans, and then threw on a sweatshirt. I ran to the back door and flung it open so Sandy could go outside when she woke up. At my front door, I tugged on some sneakers without socks, and then I was outside.

Death. That word hung in the air as I ran towards the boarding house and the unknown. Kookaburras laughed overhead, their usually cheerful cry sounding now like a portent of doom.

I reached the gothic Victorian house and turned left off the black and white mosaic tiled pathway and ran through the rose garden. The scene in the back yard at the boarding house made my blood run cold. Strewn over the dry grass and the remaining purple and red geraniums of the garden were large pieces of metal and concrete. Lying amongst the rubble was Lisa. Her husband, Greg, was on his knees next to her, weeping loudly.

"I was out here having a cigarette and looking at how dry the garden was, while talking to Lisa," he sobbed. "All of a sudden, without warning, the railing gave way, and Lisa fell."

I looked up at the balcony directly above me and saw that the Juliet balustrade was missing.

"Lord Farringdon said this would happen," Cressida wailed. Mr Buttons patted her awkwardly on her shoulder, and I in turn tried to think of something to say to console them. Truth be told, I needed to be consoled as well. What was it with the boarding house and death? And why was it that the deaths had only happened since I had come to town?

It was all so surreal. I just couldn't wrap my head around the fact that there had been another incident. I rubbed my eyes, hoping this was all a nightmare, but when I opened my eyes, the scene remained the same before me: Greg, still bent over his wife's body, and Cressida and Mr Buttons clutching each other, looking entirely distraught.

Lord Farringdon walked over to Cressida. She released Mr Buttons and bent down to pick up the cat. She put her head to his ear, and then placed him gently on the ground. He sneezed, and cat hair flew everywhere. She turned to us, her face pale even under the heavily applied make-up.

"Murder!" she pronounced.

CHAPTER 3

I stood with Cressida in the foyer as we both accepted a cup of English Breakfast tea from Mr Buttons.

"Is Greg up in his room?" Cressida asked him.

"Yes, I managed to pry him away from his poor wife," Mr Buttons said.

I shook my head. "This is horrible. Were you out in the garden when it happened, Mr Buttons?"

Mr Buttons shook his head. "No, it was too early. I heard a scream, and by the time I got out there, the woman was already lying on the ground motionless and her husband was trying to revive her."

"Why us all the time?" Cressida asked, and

although the question could certainly come off as self involved, I knew she had a point. Deaths, murders, and mysteries followed those at the boarding house, and it had only happened since I had arrived in Little Tatterford.

Before anyone could answer, Blake burst through the door, accompanied by Constable Andrews.

"Is everyone okay?" Blake asked as he stopped in front of the three of us.

"There's a deceased woman in the back yard, I'm afraid," Mr Buttons said. "Newlywed."

"Husband is here?" Blake barked.

Mr Buttons pointed up the stairs. "Yes, in his room."

"Good, keep him there. I'm going to check out the crime scene with Constable Andrews. Will you three stay here?"

"How do you know it's a crime scene?" I asked.

Blake smiled a grim smile. "With you guys, it's always a crime scene."

I had no answer to that. I watched as Blake walked towards the back of the house. Cressida, Mr Buttons, and I stood in silence until Blake returned.

"Okay, what happened?" he said, pulling off his hat and rubbing his eyes.

"Her husband, Greg, called out about half an hour ago," Cressida said. "We all rushed out, and there she was."

Blake frowned. "He was the only one out there?"

"Yes," Cressida said. "There's a no smoking policy inside the boarding house. He said he usually smokes on the Juliet balcony, but this morning he went out into the back yard to smoke. Lisa was on the balcony, and they were talking when it collapsed."

Blake wrote down everything Cressida said in a small notebook he pulled out of his breast pocket. "And he's still upstairs now?"

Cressida nodded. "Yes."

"Okay, I'm going to speak with him. You three are to stay put. Make sure no one leaves, and no one goes out back. Constable Andrews is doing some work there."

When Blake reached the top of the stairs, I turned to Cressida and Mr Buttons. "This one can't be a murder, right? It's just an accident, surely."

"If it's an accident, it's my fault," Cressida said, her voice breaking.

"It's not your fault," Mr Buttons said, patting Cressida on the back. "Sometimes accidents happen."

"She was so young." Cressida held the sleeve of her pyjama shirt to her eyes as she cried. "They were just married."

"Let's sit down," Mr Buttons suggested. We moved to the side of the wall, where a padded love seat sat next to a small table upon which was a vase of fake flowers. Mr Buttons indicated that Cressida should sit. "Do you need anything, Cressida?"

"No," she sniffled, and appeared to be about to say something, when Constable Andrews rushed through the door.

"Where's Sergeant Wessley?" he asked.

"Talking with the husband," I said. "Why?"

Before he could answer, Blake appeared at the top of the stairs.

"Sergeant, it looks like the balcony was made to fall," Constable Andrews called out. "It's missing the bolts. It looks like someone removed them."

"Let's talk in private," Blake snapped.

"Right, sorry." Constable Andrews hurried up the stairs to Blake, with the three of us on his heels. Blake and Constable Andrews walked back into the room. The door was open, but beyond there was nothing but air. The balcony had fallen away completely; there was nothing remaining.

"Look here," Constable Andrews said, crouching by the balcony and pointing. Blake crouched next to him. From my position at the doorway, I was unable to see what they were looking at.

"What is it?" Cressida asked me, peering over my shoulder.

"You're right," Blake said to Constable Andrews. "The bolts have been cleanly removed. If the balustrade had simply collapsed, part of the bolts would have remained. The weight of anyone would've been enough to make the balustrade collapse—it was just sitting there, completely unsupported."

Mr Buttons stuck his head in the room. "Wouldn't someone have been aware of someone taking all the time to remove the bolts?"

Blake shrugged. "That's one of the questions Constable Andrews and I will have to answer," he said before turning to focus his attention on me.

"*Constable Andrews and I*. Understood? Not you? Or any of you."

I held up my hands. "All right."

Greg appeared from behind the door. For a moment, I'd forgotten he was there.

The man didn't speak, but looked off into the distance before rubbing his eyes and bursting into a fresh flood of tears. "It doesn't make any sense," he said between sobs. "I didn't hear her call my name or anything before it happened. There was a strange sound, like a gate opening or something, and when I turned around, I saw her fall. I was helpless to save her." His voice rose an octave. "That should've been me! I always smoke up on the balcony every morning, but for some reason, today I wanted to look at the garden close up."

"Why?" Mr Buttons asked.

"There are protesters who are giving my company a lot of grief," Greg said. "After dealing with that sort of thing lately, I felt the need to take a minute and appreciate nature. I guess I wanted to look at the garden and be reassured that my work in town won't be detrimental to what truly matters in the world. How ironic, eh?" He looked off into the distance. "I lost my wife while focusing on things that mattered less."

I wondered why Blake was staring fixedly at Greg, but then Blake turned to me and gave me his police officer look. I stepped back into the musty corridor, followed by Cressida and Mr Buttons.

The three of us exchanged glances as Blake and Constable Andrews walked into the corridor behind us. "Cressida, you'll need to find Mr Summers another room. This room is a crime scene."

"A crime scene?" Greg gasped, as his hand flew to this throat. "My wife fell from there." He pointed to the balcony. "I was down there smoking and saw it happen. The railing gave way. No one pushed her!"

Constable Andrews held out his hand. In it were bolts and screws. "No one pushed her," he said, "but these have been unscrewed."

"Andrews!" Blake barked, and then jerked his head towards the front door. "Outside!"

Constable Andrews hurried off, while Mr Buttons took Greg by the arm. "Come with me. I'll make you a nice cup of tea," he said, picking some lint from Greg's shirt.

CHAPTER 4

"Which do you think he'd like most?" Cressida asked, trying her best to mask her worried expression. Mr Buttons and I exchanged glances.

"I'm afraid I haven't the same penchant for art as you, Cressida," Mr Buttons wisely informed her. Cressida looked put out, but turned to me and raised an expectant eyebrow.

"Oh, I, uh..." I stammered. "I like all of them, Cressida. Honestly," I lied, trying my best not to run out of the room. Cressida had invited the owner of an art gallery from a nearby town to have a look at her collection, opting to hang them all in the dining room of the boarding house to display them to him.

In a word, I would have described the art collection as "unfathomable," though that didn't quite sell the display of pure horror that was aligned in front of me. There were images of plane crashes, battlefields, train wrecks, and head-on collisions. I was astounded by two things, the main thing, of course, being the subject matter. Why Cressida opted to paint such monstrosities was well and truly beyond me, though I'd all but given up trying to understand her. Secondly, it was her sheer skill. She was truly a tremendously capable artist, held back only by her own work, stubbornly continuing to draw graphic horror scenes instead of something a sane person would buy.

"Well, I hope he shares your enthusiasm," Cressida said weakly, obviously nervous about the meeting. I wanted her to sell her art, but I didn't want to meet someone that would willingly buy it either.

"When's he due?" Mr Buttons asked.

"I don't think he's pregnant," I joked, though my peerless humour seemed lost on my friends.

"Oh, in about…" Cressida began to say before she was interrupted by the door bell. "Oh, goodness, oh no!" Cressida sputtered, running in short circles around the room. I considered for a moment that it was one of the least insane things I'd seen her do. "Okay, calm down!" Cressida yelled. "I shall answer the door presently," she stated, holding her chin up high and stomping loudly to the front door. When she arrived she took a moment to catch her breath, apparently tired from her abrupt panic attack. The door bell rang again and she answered immediately, swinging the door wide and beaming even wider.

"Oh, hello," the man outside said. He was immediately identifiable as a gallery owner: an older white man, with combed back grey hair, a terrible spray-on tan, complete with a stark grey three-piece suit. "I'm Mortimer," he said with a grin. I thought he looked more like someone who was here for Cressida's soul than her art, but he seemed to be nice enough. With a name like Mortimer, he'd probably even like her artworks. Hopefully.

"Hello!" a clearly nervous Cressida yelled in his face. "I'm Cressida. Please-come-in." She said it as one word and ran back inside, as if trying to escape him entirely. He dutifully followed and greeted Mr Buttons and me politely.

"Here it is," Cressida said, motioning to the

wall of canvases. Mortimer stood in stunned silence, or at least some kind of silence. His face was totally unmoved, showing absolutely no emotion at all, but he stood stock still for several minutes. I considered that perhaps he'd had a heart attack and died on the spot—something one could hardly blame him for—but the slow rise and fall of his chest suggested otherwise.

"I love them!" Mortimer exclaimed, beaming wide. Cressida looked like she was about to faint, and on hearing the news very nearly did so, catching herself on a chair and sitting down. "It's honestly hard for me to pick just one," Mortimer said, wildly looking at each in turn. "The colours! The composition! So much passion and movement!" he exclaimed, waving his arms about.

For a brief moment I was worried that he was doing all this as some sort of cruel joke, and then I was worried that he was serious. I wasn't sure which scared me more.

"So, you like them?" Cressida asked meekly.

"I'll certainly write up a deal!" Mortimer said excitedly, still beaming. "Oh, just wait until I show Vlad. He'll be ecstatic!"

"Vlad?" Mr Buttons said to me in a stage

whisper. "Do you think he means Vlad the Impaler?" At that, Mr Buttons guffawed.

Mortimer did not seem to notice, so taken was he by the art. I felt hysteria rising in me and I did my best to push it down. As a child, I had been overtaken by fits of laughter at inappropriate times such as someone's funeral or when I was bored in church. It happened because I was nervous, and for some reason, I was nervous now.

"I would be more than happy to take ten pieces, Cressida," Mortimer said, rubbing his hands together. "And then, according to response, we might have an exhibition."

Cressida gasped and I suppressed a nervous giggle. Perhaps Mortimer's art gallery had a clientele that wouldn't mind graphic scenes of dismembering. I sure hoped so, both for their sake and for Cressida's.

"I'll select ten paintings now, if that's all right with you."

"Yes, of course! Yes, of course," Cressida gushed. She did a little dance on the spot.

"We haven't discussed the gallery's commission yet," Mortimer said. "Anyway, it's all set out in the contract."

Cressida nodded happily and clutched her

stomach. She looked as though she was going to be sick and I hoped she wouldn't be sick all over one of her paintings. Then again, Mortimer might think that was an artistic contribution—who would know?

Mr Buttons trailed behind both Mortimer and Cressida, as Mortimer went up and down the dining room trying to find the ten paintings he thought would sell the best. At that point, Dorothy burst into the dining room. She gasped loudly when she saw us. "Who are you?" she rudely addressed Mortimer.

Before Mortimer could reply, Mr Buttons spoke up. "This gentleman is here to appraise Cressida's paintings with a view to hanging them in his gallery. Madam, would you kindly desist from your unseemly manner of conduct?"

Dorothy scowled at him. "This is no time for frivolity," she muttered darkly. "There's been a murder!" With that, she turned on her heel and hurried from the room.

Mortimer clutched his throat. "A murder?"

Mr Buttons hurried to reassure him. "That was the cook. She is, well, prone to dramatics. I expect she was talking about her cooking."

Mortimer nodded, and he and Cressida

turned their attention back to the paintings. Mr Buttons leant over and whispered loudly in my ear. "Did you see how Dorothy burst into the room? She's up to something! You mark my words."

"Well, she was acting somewhat furtively," I said, "but that doesn't mean she's a murderer."

"I have pulled many a tarot card about that woman over recent times," Mr Buttons said, "and none of them have been good. She is a murderer, and I won't be convinced otherwise."

I sighed loudly, and rubbed my forehead. When I looked up, Mr Buttons was congratulating Cressida, who was still speaking to Mortimer.

"Yes, well done, Cressida," Mr Buttons chimed in, shaking her hand furiously. "This calls for some English Breakfast tea."

Mortimer did not look impressed at the sound of English Breakfast tea. I expected he preferred a cocktail or a gin and tonic. I didn't mix in high society circles, but I assumed tea was not the favoured drink. Nevertheless, Mortimer duly followed Cressida's lead and sat down at the large cherry wood dining table. I sat opposite them, keeping the most gruesome of the paintings behind me.

We all looked at Mr Buttons expectantly. After all, he was always the one who fetched the tea. I assumed his hesitation was due to his not wanting to interact with Dorothy in the kitchen. Nevertheless, not long after Mr Buttons walked into the kitchen, I heard the outer door slam. I figured that was Dorothy on her way out.

Mr Buttons soon returned, pushing a heavy looking wooden tray mobile in front of him. He set an empty porcelain cup in front of each of us, and then produced a rather ornate teapot which he placed delicately on a porcelain stand. "It's Aynsley," he said, as if he were stating an obvious fact.

We all nodded.

Mr Buttons then placed a plate of cucumber sandwiches in the centre of the table. Just then, Greg walked into the room and suddenly stopped. "Oh, I'm so sorry. I didn't realise you had guests."

"Please join us, dear," Cressida said. "I'd like you to meet Mortimer Fyfe-Waring. Mortimer, this is Greg Summers. You've probably heard of him. He is the famous businessman responsible for the destruction of the local wilderness area."

Mr Buttons choked on his tea, and I nearly

coughed up my cucumber sandwich. What a way Cressida had with introductions!

Both Mortimer and Greg looked shocked, to say the least. Mr Buttons recovered and shot me an urgent look. I knew what he was thinking—Cressida was likely to mention that Greg's wife had been murdered, and even if she didn't, Greg himself was likely to give that away. While I personally didn't see why that would prevent Mortimer buying Cressida's paintings, it put Mr Buttons in an awkward position for not being completely honest about Dorothy's earlier remark.

Mr Buttons hurried to pour Greg a cup of tea. He accepted it, but declined a cucumber sandwich.

Unfortunately, at this point, Dorothy burst back into the room. She stood over Cressida, her hands on her hips. "I don't think there is time for the Mad Hatter's Tea Party, Miss Upthorpe, what with the recent murder!" She stormed out of the room.

"You really need to fire that woman, Cressida," Mr Buttons said. His face was beet red.

"Is she talking about her cooking again?" Mortimer asked Cressida.

I anxiously waited to hear what Cressida

would say, and I didn't have to wait long. "Oh no," Cressida said. "She's talking about the homicide, of course."

Mr Buttons shifted uncomfortably in his seat. Unperturbed, Cressida pressed on. "Dear Greg here has just experienced the murder of his poor wife, Lisa." She waved her hand expansively at Greg.

Greg dabbed at his eyes with a tissue. Mortimer was clearly at a loss. He did not say a word, but just sat there, his jaw working. For a while no one spoke, and Greg was the first to break the silence. "And the police still don't know who did it," he said angrily.

"Did it happen here at the boarding house?" Mortimer's tone bordered on disbelief.

"Yes, most surely," Cressida said.

Mortimer shot Cressida a speculative look. "And would you happen to be one of the suspects?"

Cressida nodded. "Yes, I expect I am."

Greg stood up abruptly, causing the teacups to jiggle. "I'll have to go. My apologies." And with that, he hurried out of the room.

Mr Buttons and I turned to each other and raised our eyebrows. Mortimer rubbed his hands together. "If you don't mind me saying so, this will work to our advantage for publicity. This will put up the price of your paintings, Cressida."

He stood up, and he and Cressida shook hands. Mortimer left excitedly, proclaiming that some paperwork would be on the way as soon as possible. Mr Buttons and I stood in stunned silence, not entirely sure what had transpired. It felt like waking up from some bizarre nightmare.

"Oh, I'm so happy!" Cressida announced, thrusting her hands into the air so hard that her glasses flew off, hit one of her paintings, and fell on the floor.

"Congratulations," I said, bending down to retrieve her glasses. "It looks like it all worked out."

"I'm still in shock," Cressida said, sitting down. "And I can't believe... oh, what was that?" she asked, cocking her head to one side. Lord Farringdon jumped up onto her lap and she looked at him for a time. "Yes, he was a strange sort, Lord Farringdon," she said, looking intently at her cat. I sighed, wondering if Mortimer and Cressida were part of some intricate game show made to scare me.

CHAPTER 5

It had been a long day. Cressida had invited me to dinner, and Dorothy was in her usual unpleasant mood. As soon as Dorothy had deposited the plates of Thai green curry in front of everyone and left, Mr Buttons leant over to me. "I'm sure that the murderer is Dorothy this time," he muttered. "I'm absolutely certain of it. She had a terrible fight with the victim the night before."

I sighed. "Mr Buttons, lots of people have had terrible fights with Dorothy. She hasn't murdered any of them, though."

"As far as we know," he hissed.

Eric Jefferies, one of the boarders, spoke up.

"The cops gave me the third degree," he said. "I told them about the guy across the hall from where I'm staying."

"Peter Steele?" Cressida said. "He never comes to dinner, but that doesn't make him a homicidal maniac."

I raised my eyebrows and shot Mr Buttons a helpless look. He simply shrugged and pursed his lips.

"Yes, him," Eric said, after swallowing a mouthful of rice. "The other day, when I was walking back to my room, I saw Peter Steele struggling to unlock his door while talking away on his mobile phone. I didn't hear much, but I heard enough to make me do some googling. The guy seemed irritated and said something like, 'The millionaire land developer who's tearing down the wilderness is staying at the same boarding house as I am.' I wasn't sure what he meant, so I googled it. It's pretty intriguing."

"What do you mean?" I asked him.

Eric smiled. "I found that there are various environmental groups that are unhappy with the destruction of the wilderness areas, and these groups have threatened Greg Summers. The cops were seriously interested when I told them that. Greg Summers is a big shot. He owns a commercial property development company and he's in town to destroy the wilderness area just over west of here. There are tons of protesters coming out of the woodwork, apparently. They held a rally in Tamworth recently, according to one of the sites I came across."

Eric leant across the table. "You know what I think? I think one of those protesters was trying to kill Greg Summers, and accidentally killed his wife instead."

"Trying to kill Greg?" I asked, confused.

"Maybe they weren't targeting Lisa." Eric paused before continuing. "Greg told me that he usually smokes up on the balcony, but for the first time since staying here, he decided to go out into the garden this time to have a cigarette. What if Lisa wasn't the one who was supposed to fall to her death?"

"No, Greg's poor wife, Lisa, was the intended victim," Cressida insisted. "Lord Farringdon told me that this afternoon."

Eric looked taken aback. I wondered if he knew that Lord Farringdon was Cressida's fat tabby and white cat. At any rate, he did not comment on that, but pressed on. "What if the murderer was Peter Steele? He had the motive and he had the opportunity. Greg Summers himself told me only a few hours ago that he always leant over the railing every morning to smoke a cigarette."

"I think the kid's onto something," Dorothy said, and everyone jumped. I shrieked, and my fork flew out of my hand. I had no idea she'd come into the room.

Dorothy glared at me, and continued talking. "The bolts were removed and tossed onto the ground. Greg, the husband, has admitted that his daily routine included standing on that very balcony, and now we have a possible motive. I think it's safe to surmise that someone might be trying to kill Mr Summers." With that, she picked up the fork and waved it at me in a belligerent manner, before hurrying out of the room.

"That's the most Dorothy's ever said at one time," Mr Buttons said in a stage whisper. "She's trying to throw suspicion off herself."

"You're all wrong," Cressida said in a petulant voice. "Lord Farringdon said that Lisa was the intended victim; I tell you!"

I sighed, and rubbed my temples.

I hadn't even finished my Thai green curry, when there was a loud bang on the front door followed by the bell ringing incessantly. Cressida jumped to her feet and headed for the front door, with me hard on her heels.

Cressida opened the front door to reveal a short, portly man, who was sporting an enormous, uneven, walrus-like moustache made out of brown and grey, bristly hairs.

"Are you the owner?" the man with the moustache asked in a brusque tone.

"Yes," Cressida said. "What can I do for you?"

"I am Franklin Greer, from the Little Tatterford and Shire Council," the man announced proudly. He smelt strongly of stale aftershave, which he had clearly applied by the bucket load.

"What is this about?" Mr Buttons asked. He stepped forward, and then took both edges of the man's moustache in his hands, and levelled it.

The man's jaw fell open, and he stood silent for a moment. "We got a call about a fallen balcony," he said after an interval. "I believe someone has died, have they not?"

"Yes," Cressida said again.

"I have a duty of care to all persons in workplaces, including workers and volunteers, contractors and their workers, visitors and the general public. I have to make decisions about health and safety." Franklin Greer puffed out his chest. "The Little Tatterford and Shire Council has an obligation to ensure that people are not exposed to hazards or damage. I need to see this balcony."

"It's a crime scene," I said. "It looks like someone made it collapse on purpose."

"Well, the authorities and I will decide that," the man said, a rather smug look upon his face as he curled his plump lips into a slimy smile. "But as of right now, we need everyone up and out of the boarding house."

"Why?" Cressida demanded.

The man looked her right in the eye. "Because this place is going to be shut down. It's unsafe."

"It's not unsafe," I said. "The police are treating it as a crime scene, so what does the council have to do with anything?"

"Let me assure you, madam," Franklin Greer said, his eyes narrowing, "I know my job quite well, and I know what's going on. I assume you don't know my job as well as I do, so if you please, prepare everyone to leave the boarding house."

"Are you saying it's not structurally safe?" Cressida asked.

Franklin Greer sneered. "There's been a death from a collapsed balcony. It's plain to me that the boarding house is unsafe and violates several local building codes. I need to examine the entire building and grounds."

This man was getting on my last nerve. "The police just labelled the investigation as a homicide, so how can you even think to blame the fall on the building itself?" I snapped. "The police seem to think someone took the screws and bolts out of the balustrade."

Franklin Greer smiled, a thin-lipped, nasty smile, and waved a chubby hand at us. "Prepare for the boarding house to be condemned," he said. "Good day."

Cressida shut the door with a little more force than necessary, and leant against it. "What are we going to do?" Her voice came out as a wail, so much so, that Lord Farringdon appeared from nowhere and let out a mournful howl.

"I'm not sure." I sighed long and hard.

Mr Buttons took out a white, linen handkerchief and polished the brass door knob. "We have to solve the case," he said. "Cressida, they can't shut you down and place the blame on the building if the police solve the case. We just have to make sure they find out what really happened. When the case is solved, the boarding house will be completely in the clear."

CHAPTER 6

The woman had the stereotypical, hard-as-nails secretary look down pat. Her hair was short and sleek. Her blouse was form fitting, perhaps a little too much so, and her sharp, black slacks showed off her long legs and ended at the ankle. She stood as if she were in command of the world, not an assistant to a land developer.

I smiled at the imposing woman. I figured she was the sort who didn't know what the word *no* meant. It was difficult to envision her as an assistant to anyone.

"Would you explain why you're here again?" I asked in an apologetic tone, ignoring the impatient grumbling of the woman in front of me. I had a mental image of her with a drum and a whip, mercilessly keeping a score of office clerks working non stop on their projects.

"As I said, I am Greg's *personal* assistant," the woman said in a haughty tone.

Oh yes, so much more important than a normal assistant. Thankfully, I managed to stop myself saying that aloud.

"I just got into town, and I have an urgent document for Greg to sign. It can't wait." The woman's voice was authoritative. She fixed the front of the boarding house with a critical frown.

Some personal assistant. She didn't act as if she knew that Greg was on his honeymoon, much less that his wife had just died. She did not appear the least bit apologetic that she was about to disturb him at one of the most inappropriate times possible. I let out a long sigh of resignation. "Please come in, and I'll see if Greg is taking visitors right now. He just lost his wife, so…"

"Yes," she snapped, cutting me off. "I'm well aware of that. And he is expecting me." The woman brushed past me.

I shrugged. At least I'd tried. If Greg wished to speak with a drill sergeant in secretary's clothing, it wasn't any of my business. People had their own ways of dealing with grief.

By the time I caught up to the woman, I found Cressida blocking the stairway to the upper floor, demanding to know the woman's identity.

Cressida's arms were waving in the air. "I don't care if you're a Nobel Prize winner with a cure for typhoid! You get your high heels and high horse into that living room and wait until I talk to Greg. Unless he tells me he is expecting company, I'm not going to have a guest bothered."

The woman could have killed with the glare she gave Cressida, but before she could speak, Greg appeared at the top of the stairs, looking tired and apologetic. He regarded his guest unhappily. "It's all right. I was just coming down to tell you that I was expecting Julie to come by."

I had the distinct impression the woman had only been expected when she had pulled up in the driveway. Cressida moved to the side, scooting around Julie as she stomped up the stairs.

"Let me know if you need anything, Greg," Cressida called up. "Dinner will be in a couple hours. Did you want it delivered to your room?"

"If you would, please, Cressida."

"Will you need a second plate for your guest?"

"No, Julie will be leaving very shortly," Greg said, as he nudged the woman out of his personal space.

I did not blame him at all. I would hate to have work hunt me down at such a time. I did feel a slight pang of guilt for enjoying the look of shock and disappointment on Greg's personal assistant's face when he said she would be leaving shortly.

I turned my attention to Cressida, as the pair disappeared around the corner of the stairway to make their way to Greg's room. Cressida looked exhausted.

"Is everything okay, Cressida?" I said, as I guided her towards the dining room. "Would you like me to make some coffee?"

"Oh, if only coffee were the solution," Cressida sighed, but she managed a weak, grateful smile and nodded. A pot was already brewed and looked fairly fresh. I added extra sugar to the two mugs, and then returned to the dining room.

"So what happened?" I asked, as I took a sip of my drink.

"Oh my, what's happened?" Cressida

exclaimed, as she rubbed her temples with the flat of her hand. "I've already blocked two reporters trying to get a look at Greg and the railing and stuff. And then before I finished breakfast, the horrible council man came back with an inspector, and threatened to shut the place down."

"But Blake thinks that the railing was tampered with," I said. "They can't blame you for that."

Cressida drained half her cup before speaking. "It's not just that. He said they've had multiple reports of safety and sanitation violations. They're going to do a major inspection in a few days. If we don't pass, the boarding house is done. He'll shut us down."

My hand flew to my mouth. "But who was complaining? All the online reviews have nothing but praise for the place."

"One person in particular. A Cynthia Devonshire." Cressida grimaced and stared into her cup. "The inspector that the horrid little man, Franklin Greer, brought with him knows Dorothy. They're in the church choir together. He told Dorothy that Cynthia Devonshire was the one who'd made the complaints."

I dug through my memory, trying to remember anyone by the name of Cynthia, but try as I might, I could not remember the name at all. "Who is she?"

Cressida finished off her coffee and tapped the bottom of the cup on the table. "Cynthia Devonshire's the owner of that new Bed and Breakfast on the other side of town."

I swatted myself on the forehead. Cynthia Devonshire was going after business aggressively, and had gone so far as to put a flyer advertising her B&B in my mailbox.

Cressida was still talking. "Of course, it's simply a matter of a business harassing a rival, but Franklin Greer doesn't care. He didn't even care when I said that she's never even set foot in this place. He kept saying that all complaints have to be treated as valid, and so we'll be inspected to see if we should be open at all."

"That's awful!" I shook my head. I had never imagined that a B&B would be such a cut throat business. I would have thought there would be plenty of clients to go around. I was appalled that Cynthia Devonshire would use a tactic as ugly as sending inspectors to harass and shut down the competition.

"There's a lover's quarrel raging upstairs!"

I jumped. I'd been so lost in thought that I hadn't noticed Mr Buttons entering the dining room.

"A lover's quarrel?" Cressida asked, looking confused and at the end of her wits.

"Yes. I imagine the man would have quite a lot of explaining to do, well, if his wife were around to explain things to, at least," Mr Buttons said, in an irritated tone. He gave us a pleading look. "Please don't send me back up there, ladies. I've no stomach for listening to a soap opera through my bedroom wall."

"Wait. What's going on?" Cressida asked. She waved Mr Buttons to sit down and explain.

"Whoever just came in to pay this Greg fellow a visit is quite a vocal woman. She's going on and on about how they are meant to be. He's yelling about her trying to crawl into his bed after his wife has just died. Both are yelling about how he did or did not play games with her."

My jaw fell open. "Are you serious?"

Mr Buttons nodded, and then he mimicked a stern voice. "How dare you, woman! My wife is not even cold in the ground and you are trying to crawl into my bed?"

He leant back in his chair and crossed his arms. "Then she said she loved him. He called her a desperate... well, it's not a word I would ever repeat. It's one you have heard many a time, though, Sibyl."

My expression must have shown my confusion, as Mr Buttons continued, "From your foul-mouthed cockatoo," he said.

I nodded.

"Anyway, at that point, I think she might have slapped him. I was heading out my door about then, so I couldn't say for certain."

"My goodness!" Cressida pushed herself up from the table, and Mr Buttons laid his hand on her arm.

"Just let them get it out of their system, Cressida. No good comes from getting into those spats, and no one else is around for them to bother."

At that moment, we heard the click-clack of heels on the polished tallow wood floorboards, heading loudly in the direction of the front door. Soon after, the door slammed.

Mr Buttons winced at the sound. "Well now, at least if she damaged the hinges we know where to send the bill." He rearranged the coffee cups on the table so that they all made a straight line.

"I should have known it was her. That nagging, shrill voice is hard to forget."

"You've met her before?" I asked.

"Oh yes. Well, not directly, but I did see her at the Bistro yesterday afternoon. She was doing her level best to reduce a poor waitress to tears over not refilling her glass fast enough, and then she said something about her food not being to her taste, too."

"Are you sure?" I asked. "She said she just got into town today."

Mr Buttons shook his head. "There is no doubt it was her. I won't forget that voice or face any time soon."

Cressida and I looked at each other, and then Cressida got back to her feet. "I better go check and make sure everything is all right. Mr Buttons, I'm sorry they disturbed you."

"Think nothing of it. It's not the first spat I've witnessed." Mr Buttons waved off the apology as he made his way towards the kitchen. "Would either of you care for English Breakfast tea?"

"No, thanks," Cressida said, as she made her way upstairs.

"Sibyl?" Mr Buttons turned his attention to me.

I lifted my half empty coffee cup and gave it a little shake. "It's coffee."

"One of these days I'll have to break that machine," Mr Buttons said, as he shook his head in disgust.

CHAPTER 7

I strolled up to the boarding house, wondering why Mr Buttons had not turned up to walk Sandy with me that morning. Our arrangement was that if he wasn't there on time, I would proceed without him, but he was there most days.

As soon as I walked through the front door, Cressida hurried over to me. "Greg woke up to find his car vandalised. I was just on the phone with Blake. He's coming right over."

While I was pleased that I would see Blake again so soon, I wasn't happy that Greg's car had been vandalised. The poor man, after everything he'd been through.

Cressida pointed out the front door and

slightly to the right. "Go and take a look for yourself. He parks over in that corner. It's the silver BMW."

I walked out the door with Cressida, and over to the parking area. "Wow," I said. "Wow." There was no other word for it, really.

The front driver-side tyre was flattened, and what appeared to be the handle of a switchblade jutted from the rubber. I walked around the car and saw that all four tyres had been slashed. The most dramatic vandalism was in the form of large, red letters which were scrawled across the side of the car. The dark red, blood-like colour filled me with a sense of dread. I squinted to try to understand the word. "What does that even mean?" I asked myself aloud. A single word filled the length of the sedan: HOOW.

"What does HOOW mean?" I asked Cressida.

Cressida shrugged. "I don't have a clue. Mr Buttons seems to think it's some sort of acronym or abbreviation or something of the sort."

"He thinks each letter represents a separate word?" I thought about it. What could each of the letters mean? H. O. O. W. "Could it be a typo?" I asked Cressida.

Cressida chuckled. "People only make typos on computers," she said.

"Oh, yes." I felt silly for saying it, but I was caffeine-deprived.

I leant over and peered at the letters, trying to think what the acronym could spell. There were so many possibilities for H alone: Hearts, Honour, Honesty, Hate, Hands.

"Hands Off Our Wilderness," a familiar voice said.

I swung around to see Blake walking up to me. "That's what HOOW means? So it's the protesters Greg mentioned?"

"That's the likely conclusion, that it has something to do with that environmental protest against the wilderness area being developed. It's probably their group name."

"Do you think this vandalism might be connected to Lisa's, err, fall?"

Blake looked grim. "Anything is possible, Sibyl. We're going to take some photographs of the vehicle, and then have it towed to the impound lot for testing."

"Testing? What kind of testing?" I prodded.

"Fingerprints mainly. If the knife doesn't have

any, the car itself might. We just need a name, anything to jumpstart this investigation."

Mr Buttons walked up, with Greg following at a short distance. "Hello, Blake."

Blake greeted him with a nod. "Like I was just telling Sibyl, we're going to see if we can find some leads, and then we'll take it from there."

"Do you think the same person that did this could have tampered with that balcony railing?" Mr Buttons asked.

Blake nodded. "It's definitely possible, but until we have a suspect in our sights, it's impossible to know for sure either way. I'll need to speak to Greg."

Blake took Greg aside and the two of them spoke. I stood with Cressida and Mr Buttons as the three of us watched the conversation from afar. Their words were unintelligible at this distance, but I got the impression that it wasn't a fun chat. Greg threw his arms around, and a deep frown was on his face. Every now and then, Greg yelled. Blake had his back to me, but I could tell that his shoulders were tense.

"Look at him," Cressida said. "I understand Greg's having a very bad time, but he can't just go around treating everyone like that, simply because he's frustrated." Cressida was clearly beyond annoyed at the situation.

"I feel sorry for him," I said. "He's just trying to cope. Then, on top of everything else, his car gets damaged. I hope they catch whoever did it. This is really starting to make me believe that Lisa's fall was deliberate."

Greg hurried to the house, half walking and half running, and Blake headed back to the three of us.

"It took a bit, but he's finally calm," Blake said. "I explained to him what we'll be testing the car and knife for, and that we're trying to rule out any possibility that the property damage and death of his wife are related. I feel for the guy. It must be tough to deal with."

"I bet," I added.

"Well, I'm going to head back to the station and see what's up. It should only be a few hours or so until we find out if there are any usable prints."

After Blake left, I returned to my cottage to fuel with caffeine. "You're an ugly %&$% fool," my sulphur-crested cockatoo squawked at me as I walked in the door.

I pulled a face at him and took him outside.

"You're depriving a village of a *^&$ idiot," he said, as I firmly shut the back door on him.

I switched on my coffee machine, and leant over it to inhale the heavenly scent of coffee. I had the beginnings of a headache, but nothing that two Advil, three cups of coffee, and six large spoons of sugar all up wouldn't fix.

I propped myself up on the cushions on my sofa and sipped my coffee. Aha. I sighed blissfully as my caffeine levels rose to the required minimum. My bliss turned to irritation as I thought about my rude, trash-talking cockatoo. He had been such a lovely cockatoo before my horrible ex-husband, Andrew, had taught him to say rude things. What's more, Andrew had plotted to murder me, and was managing to delay my property settlement from his jail cell.

My stomach clenched when my phone rang. I jumped and spilled some coffee on my jeans. "Is anyone else dead?" I blurted into the phone.

"Hello," a disembodied voice said. "Does your roof need cladding? We have a special on at the moment and can offer you a very good deal. Our product is visually attractive and has a timeless appeal, and comes in a range of colours."

I groaned. Not another sales call. I tried to interrupt two or three times, but then hung up.

The phone rang immediately, and this time, I checked the caller I.D. before answering. Cressida.

"Hello," I said politely. "I hope this isn't bad news."

"No," came Cressida's voice. "Blake's here, and he's arrested someone for the vandalism. Do you want to come up?"

I arrived in the sitting room at the boarding house at the same time as Mr Buttons.

"Who did it?" Mr Buttons asked.

"Quinten Masters," Blake said. "He goes by the name *The Environmentalist* online. The guy runs a website that's dedicated to this sort of thing." Blake looked around before continuing. "He has a popular blog about the destruction of wilderness areas. The guy's one of those protesters we keep hearing about, just like I suspected."

"Did Quinten confess or make any statements?" I asked.

Blake shook his head. "None at all. He lawyered up right away, but that's not all too surprising. He's young and has a clean record. Hitting him with the vandalism charges won't be tough, but trying to connect him to a murder is another matter entirely. At this stage in the game it is, at least."

"Are you sure his motive for the damage to Greg's car involves the wilderness preservation and all that?" Mr Buttons asked, producing a spray bottle and a cleaning rag from a plastic bag and scrubbing at a dirty mark on the window.

"We're not positive, but we can't see any other possible motive. He has a popular blog with thousands of followers. My tech guy was telling me that Quinten Masters posted about the vandalism earlier today and said that Greg had gotten what he deserved, but deleted the post once a few people commented to complain about his attitude. Luckily, when someone deletes information in the digital age, there are always ways to retrieve it."

"So, if these people are trying to stop Greg's destruction of the wilderness area, why would they be personally attacking him instead of tying themselves to trees or something more productive?" I asked. "He's not the only one in the company."

"That's a good question, Sibyl," Blake said. "I wish I knew the answer. All I was told was that the blog has been mentioning Greg for the last couple months at least, saying he's the one responsible for the company's plans to destroy the wilderness area. If these crimes are related to this whole environmental issue, I have a feeling HOOW and this website have been playing a large role in what the perpetrator or perpetrators have been doing."

"It seems possible, but overly complicated," Mr Buttons added, "but would someone want to murder someone to protect a wilderness area?"

"Welcome to law enforcement," Blake said with a smile. "You never know what you're going to have to deal with when you wake up and come into work."

"That sounds like my job," Cressida said.

Blake shrugged. "I'm going to head back and look at the evidence from both cases. I want to see if there aren't some points of comparison or any clues that can link Lisa's fall to Quinten's wilderness movement." He smiled at me, and then made his way towards the exit.

"I can kind of understand trashing someone's car and painting your slogan on their window, but removing some bolts so someone gets killed? It just seems a bit on the extreme side of things, don't you think?" I said.

Mr Buttons and Cressida both looked at me, but no one spoke for a while.

The silence was finally broken by Mr Buttons. "Maybe there's more to it than just wilderness protection and preservation."

"What do you mean?" I asked.

"I don't know. Maybe the land is special to the person or something. I'm just saying that I think it's possible that the murderer might hold a grudge of some sort. If there's enough hatred towards something or someone, you'd be surprised at how far some people would go to eliminate it."

Cressida interrupted him. "That's crazy talk. I don't think Lord Farringdon would agree with you."

"I think we're all just mentally exhausted," I said, noticing an offended look on Mr Buttons' face. "I guess anything's possible, Mr Buttons, but until Blake catches a lead, we're just barking up empty trees."

Mr Buttons smiled wanly. "All right. I have some reading I need to get done tonight, but if I'm needed for anything, I'm just a call away."

"I might take you up on that, Mr Buttons," Cressida said.

"If you have any more problems with Greg,

don't try to calm him down. Just call me." I addressed that comment to Cressida.

"Thank you. I don't like trying to calm him down," she said softly.

"I know. It does him no good to be so loud and aggressive, especially towards you and any of the others who are trying to help."

"In all honesty, it's not because I don't want to listen to him rant and rave. It's because he scares me at times." Cressida leant closer and her eyes widened. "And Lord Farringdon told me that Greg seemed more upset when he saw his car than when his wife fell from the balcony."

CHAPTER 8

I sighed as I checked my watch. I had been in some traffic jams in my day, but this was ridiculous!

I leant my head out the window and tried to see the road ahead. I didn't see any signs of smoke or an accident, and there was no scream of emergency sirens. What else would bring the highway traffic to a complete standstill? This usually only happened once a year in Little Tatterford, at the Festival, but there were always detour signs then.

I checked my watch again as I leant back into the car. Those fifteen seconds since the last watch check felt like two minutes, at least. I suppressed a groan and looked at the stack of folders on the seat beside me. I supposed I could attempt to go over my paperwork. There was definitely no shortage. I had my grooming schedule to organise, and my finances, such as they were, to balance.

The nearest coffee shop was only a car length away from me. Just a few feet separated me from the limbo of cars with their out of state license plates. If I could inch my way in, I could get coffee and wait for the traffic to start flowing again.

Firstly, I needed to get off the road and park. At this rate, it would be an hour before traffic moved enough for me to inch that close. I looked forlornly at the entrance of the coffee shop taunting me. Would I get into trouble if I just edged up that nice, grassy incline into the driveway? Yes, most likely; Blake would give me an earful for certain.

As I was contemplating my next move to escape traffic jam purgatory, the traffic started to move again, albeit ever so slowly.

I had no idea if whatever was blocking the traffic was gone, but regardless, I was now looking forward to a coffee fix, and this coffee shop had wonderful caramel slices.

No sooner had I gotten out of my car than I heard the sound of a ruckus. I was halfway across the parking lot when someone slammed into me, causing me to stumble several steps and drop my purse on the pavement. "Hey!" I exclaimed.

I whirled around as two people made a mad dash across the road. I crouched down and started to collect my things. I picked up my purse and the change that had fallen out of it, and stuffed it back in. They could have at least tried to avoid crashing into people if they didn't plan to help clean up the mess. A quick sorry would have been nice.

I swung back around, when a uniformed police officer grabbed me by the arm. I hadn't seen him before—he must have been from out of town. "You're being taken in for disturbing the peace and blocking traffic," he said.

I tried to pull away, out of instinct, but his grip tightened. "But I'm a local," I said. "I got caught in traffic, so I parked, and went to get coffee. And those people ran past me and knocked my stuff all over the ground."

The police officer's expression was grim. "I've had enough of you protesters," he said. "Your friends got away, but you won't." And with that, he firmly guided me down the road.

"I'm just an innocent bystander," I said. "Those people ran into me. I didn't even know there was a protest."

The police officer stuffed me into his vehicle and drove me to the police station. It was all so surreal, and had happened so quickly. Next thing I knew, I was sitting opposite the man in an interview room, telling him yet again what had happened.

"Do you have anyone who can corroborate your story?" he asked, making me want to bang my head on the desk between us.

"How about half a town?" a familiar voice said with open irritation. "Sibyl Potts is a local resident."

"That fact doesn't explain her being at the scene."

Blake pointed a finger under the man's nose. "And so were fifty or so locals, and innocent people driving down the highway. You do realise that Little Tatterford is half way between Sydney and Brisbane, don't you? You arrested at least three locals." Blake walked around the table and helped me up. "She's being released, effective immediately."

"Now see here!"

That was all the man had time to say, before Blake lowered his face to the man's. "I haven't seen such incompetence in a long time. Rest assured, I will report your behaviour. I don't know how you do things where you come from, but you're in the wrong jurisdiction to be doing it."

I gawked as Blake escorted me towards the door. I had seen Blake upset before, when there had been a tough case, when I had poked my nose into police matters, even when umpires had unfairly awarded free kicks against his football team, but this made all those seem minor. I could not remember ever seeing him this angry. The out-of-town police officer did not seem ready to test his luck. He sat there mutely as Blake and I left.

As soon as we were out of the room, Blake took a long breath. "Are you all right? Sibyl?" Blake asked again, tilting his head to the side. "I asked if you were okay?"

"I just wanted a cup of coffee." I felt tears well up the instant I spoke, making me turn red. I gave a short, nervous laugh, as I blotted my eyes with the back of my hand. "I'm fine; I'm fine," I muttered.

Blake gave me a kind smile and put his arm around my shoulders. "Well, if you have a minute, I could treat you to some blacker-than-black coffee with extra sugar to hide the char. I'd take you to a café, but I'm too busy with the protest rally in town."

I thanked him and sat on a blue, plastic chair in the police station staff room. "The protest rally. It's HOOW, isn't it?"

Blake nodded. "It's them, all right. They started off peacefully enough, but then it quickly deteriorated into people sitting in the middle of the highway and choking traffic. The cops who were called in to help keep the peace weren't organised for dealing with any real trouble." Blake sighed. "They've made the situation worse by grabbing random people off the streets."

I didn't have long to talk to Blake as he was called back to the rally, and I hightailed it out of there as fast as I could. Luckily, the traffic was now moving, so I was able to drive back to my cottage. I parked, but instead of going inside, I hurried back to the boarding house in search of some friend therapy, which sounded pretty good to me right then. I'd even let Mr Buttons make me some English Breakfast tea if he offered. And if anyone could make me laugh about getting arrested when trying to get coffee, Cressida could.

As soon as I walked through the door, I heard the unhappy noise of Dorothy slamming cabinet doors and banging pots and pans. I knew that sound only too well; that was the sound of a special menu request. There must be a new guest tonight.

"Oh Sibyl," Cressida called cheerfully as she made her way to me. "We have six travellers who just checked in. They're here for some sort of community outreach rally."

My face fell, and I let out a groan. "Oh, is that what they called it? No Cressida, they're members of HOOW."

I explained the situation in detail. By the time I was finished, Cressida was open mouthed, Mr Buttons had joined us and was shaking his head, and even Dorothy had stopped banging to gawk in shock around the door.

"My goodness, you'd better get Blake something nice for coming to your rescue like that!" Cressida exclaimed. "So they were the ones who blocked up traffic today?"

"Yes, and they're the ones who are opposing Greg destroying the wilderness."

"Greg's destruction of the wilderness area most certainly should be opposed," Cressida said, and Mr Buttons and I agreed. "Yet that's no excuse for someone murdering Greg's wife."

Mr Buttons rubbed his chin thoughtfully. "There's one thing that concerns me though, ladies."

"That HOOW vandalised Greg's car and blocked traffic?" I asked.

"Well, yes. That too."

"That Blake got away with chewing out another cop?" Cressida asked hesitantly.

"I'm surprised he didn't clock the man a good one, actually. But no."

"Well what?" Cressida asked impatiently.

Mr Buttons pointed up at the second floor. "We have the activists and the man they hate sleeping under the one roof."

CHAPTER 9

I was at one of the cafés in town, having coffee with Cressida. The café was a cute little place with an interior design scheme modelled after an old-fashioned café. "Do you think this place has been around longer than the boarding house?" I asked Cressida.

Cressida considered my question for a moment, and then shrugged. "Probably, though I can't say for sure. It's designed to look old, but it might've been here for a fraction of the time."

Cressida had suggested we have coffee in town as a respite from the recent days' events, but I couldn't help but feel sad. I poured some sugar into my coffee and thought about Lisa. No matter how hard I tried, erasing the memory seemed to be impossible. The name of every possible suspect reeled through my mind like an old film being pulled through a projector. I was unable to pinpoint a most likely suspect.

"So, Cressida," I said, "do you have any idea as to who could be behind Lisa's death?" I spoke in a soft tone. "Of course Mr Buttons is sure it's Dorothy, but he suspects her of every murder." As soon as I said the words *every murder*, I felt sadder than ever. There had been several murders since I'd moved to Little Tatterford. I had even forgotten the precise number.

Cressida tapped her chin. "I was kind of starting to suspect Dorothy myself. She did have that awful fight with Lisa the night before she died."

I shot her a curious look. "Yes, I heard that, but with everything else going on, I forgot about it."

"Lisa asked Dorothy to cook the meat a little bit longer than she had. I get complaints about Dorothy from time to time, but most people don't go to the lengths of going into the kitchen to complain to Dorothy in person," she said. "Oh, speaking of complaints, it's Cynthia Devonshire. Don't look now."

I looked up to see a young, attractive woman, overdressed for the local town, strolling into the café. She was. She flung her long, blonde hair extensions over her shoulder at least three times before she reached us.

"Shush. I said, 'Don't look now.'" Cressida pressed her lips against her finger.

Cynthia Devonshire approached our table. "Hello, Cressida. How have you been?" Her lips were tightly pursed, and she spoke in a posh, affected accent, drawing out her vowels.

Cressida shifted uncomfortably in her seat. "Fine, thanks, and you?"

"I thought you would have been most upset after the dreadful accident at your establishment," the pretentious woman continued.

"It was no accident," Cressida retorted. "It was murder!"

The woman looked down her long, pointed nose at Cressida. "I do keep hearing that the police suspect foul play, but where is the proof of such a ridiculous claim?"

"Excuse me?" Cressida said. "The proof is in the fact that my building is completely up to date, and there haven't been any reported code violations or injuries on my property."

The woman smiled thinly or sneered. I couldn't tell which. "Oh come on. That's preposterous. Who would know someone was going to be leaning against a specific railing on a specific balcony, and on a specific day? If this ends up being solved as a murder, we need to crown the suspect a genius. His planning abilities and level of strategic accuracy should be commended, if he managed to kill his target in such a clever way."

Cressida's frustration seemed to be boiling over. I kept nudging her with my elbow, but to no avail.

"When the police catch the guy and lock him away, I'll be expecting an apology directly from you!" Cressida exclaimed. "You can applaud the murderer's planning skills if you wish, but he or she's a sick person and you're a sick woman. It's terrible that you're using a tragedy such as this to get a financial advantage for your business!"

"Think what you wish," Cynthia Devonshire said in a snarky tone. "*I* have taken no steps to using that poor woman's demise for my own benefit. If I'm guilty of anything at all, it's of reporting a shoddy boarding house run by someone who doesn't know how to keep her guests safe."

"Reporting?" I repeated. "What are you talking about?"

The woman fixed her gaze upon me. "Well, I hear it's been going around town that the boarding house will be inspected soon. After learning about that horrific accident, I felt it was my moral obligation to make sure the local council knew of the structural deficiencies of such an old dirty facility."

Cressida shook. "So, you're admitting that you falsely reported my B&B?"

A smug look decorated the woman's otherwise expressionless face. "I didn't falsely report anything. You can tell from yards away that those balconies need to be renovated. I've spoken to former guests of yours who did nothing but complain about the lack of amenities and how things are always crazy over there." The woman once again flipped her hair extensions from her face. "I don't want there to be any animosity between us, Ms Upthorpe, but I cannot approve of you cutting corners and endangering lives."

"Thank you for your concern," Cressida said in a syrupy, false voice. "I'll make sure I look into your concerns and resolve them by any means necessary." Cressida smiled so widely that deep crevices formed in her thick makeup.

Cynthia Devonshire stood silent for a moment, and then flipped her hair once more and stormed to the counter.

"Nice one," I said.

Cressida smiled weakly. "I always hate it when people who should be mad at me are nice. I figured it might work on her, so I tested it out."

I smiled. "Looks like it worked like a charm. I know she's purposely trying to provoke you, but with everything that's going on, we need to be careful and worry about protecting ourselves."

"I know that, Sibyl," Cressida continued. "It's just so irritating when you hear about accusations being made, and you know it's all lies, but there's nothing you can do to prove it."

I nodded. "Anyway, back to Dorothy. Do you really think she could possibly harm someone?"

Cressida bit her bottom lip and frowned. "I think anything is possible. Sometimes, the least likely person is the most obvious culprit. People just don't realise it because the clues are there to point you in the wrong direction."

"Since when have you been an amateur sleuth?" I asked.

"I'm far from that," Cressida said. "I just know how far people are usually willing to go when they feel like everything is on the line. Sometimes nothing will stop them from achieving their goals."

I understood only too well. After all, my ex-husband had plotted to kill me with the help of his mistress.

"Anyway," Cressida continued, "I don't really suspect Dorothy. I don't know who else it could be, though. Well, other than that environmental activist or whatever he is, but murdering someone seems a bit extreme for such a noble cause."

"That's true," I agreed.

Cynthia Devonshire, coffee in hand, walked back past our table. "I will be seeing you again in the near future, I would assume."

"I look forward to it," Cressida said evenly.

"I wouldn't be looking forward to anything if I were you," the woman said. "Either we'll end up putting you out of business, or you'll end up going bankrupt when your decrepit building falls apart and hurts someone again."

CHAPTER 10

"Leave it to us to have a paperwork party," Cressida said as she took a sip of her drink, and then shuffled the files she was updating.

"We're unconventional and adventurous like that." I smiled and sighed as I looked at my own untamed tangle of forms and receipts.

Cressida and I were sitting in the dining room with our paperwork spread out around the table. We had both fallen behind, and so Cressida suggested we should sit together to catch up. It was ironic that trying to organise receipts was the most relaxing part of my week. Part of me hoped that Mr Buttons would join us, but that wouldn't help with the paperwork.

Greg poked his head around the door. "Good evening, ladies."

I returned his greeting, while Cressida waved. Greg looked like the whole ordeal was wearing him down. While it did not show in his appearance, his manner was sad and less energetic than usual.

"How are things going?" I asked him.

"The environmentalists have made it worse," he said sadly.

While I certainly did not approve of Greg destroying the wilderness area, I could not help but feel sorry for him. His wife had just died, and he had possibly been the intended murder victim. To make matters worse, the media kept calling him for a statement, and then he had to contend with his aggressive personal assistant. Cressida had to put the six protesters in a separate wing and organise special meal times, all to keep them and Greg from running into each other.

'No matter how frustrating life is, someone always has it worse,' my grandfather used to say whenever I complained about anything. He was a wise man. I wouldn't switch places with Greg for a million dollars.

"What are you ladies up to?" Greg nodded at the table full of scattered files and calculators.

"Paperwork party," Cressida explained, as she waved a hand grandly over the spread out mess. "I'd ask if you wanted to join in," she said as a joke.

"Actually, I might have to take you up on that offer." Greg rubbed the back of his neck. "With what happened to Lisa, it's been hard to stay on track with work."

A knock interrupted our conversation. Cressida waved Greg to sit down, while she went to check on the door.

"So, how are you doing?" I asked in the awkward silence that followed Cressida's departure.

"One day at a time." Greg sighed. "Just a little bit more to go, and then I'll take some time off."

As I tried to find the right words to express my sympathy for his situation, two men made their way into the room.

Greg looked up. "I've been expecting you, Detectives."

Cressida and I left the dining room to give them privacy.

"Never a dull day." Cressida sighed and rubbed the back of her neck.

"It will be all right," a familiar voice assured her.

Blake! I couldn't remember ever being so happy to see him. It felt so good to see him standing there with a cup of coffee in his hand.

"What are they here for?" I asked him, nodding in the direction of the dining room.

Before he could answer, Greg's voice bellowed, making the three of us jump. "What do you mean, no suspects?"

The three of us exchanged glances, as Greg continued to yell. "How about twenty six environmentalists breathing down my neck? Half of them are so extreme they'd sell off their mother to save a wombat! What about the rival companies? The historic preservation group? Those loons claiming the land has been in their family for hundreds of years? Do I need to draw you idiots a map? What are my tax dollars paying you for? My wife is dead, and you think someone killed her. And you have no clue who might have done it?"

"Sir, please calm down."

"I've been calm! I've been sitting on my hands wondering when you were going to take care of this mess! Get out! Get out, and let me know when you actually have some answers!"

Cressida made a move towards the door, but Blake placed a hand on her shoulder and shook his head.

After Greg ranted and raved some more, the detectives walked out of the room and headed for the front door of the boarding house. There was a banging sound inside the room, followed by the sound of rustling papers. Cressida and I hurried into the room, followed by Blake.

"Greg!" Cressida snapped. She crouched to gather the papers on the floor. "This isn't *your* office!"

Greg stopped his frantic pacing of the room. He mumbled an apology, and then bent over to pick up Cressida's things and return them to the table.

"I know this is a hard time for you, Greg, but be more careful!" Cressida scolded, shaking her head.

"I'm sorry. They came all the way here to tell me that my wife was murdered, and they haven't a clue by whom." Greg again paced the room furiously. "As if I didn't already know that!"

I sighed and tried to get the paperwork organised without reading too much of Cressida's personal information.

"There's a strong likelihood that you were the target," Blake said, as he helped collect the papers. "In fact, you could still be targeted as we speak."

"Really, now?" Greg asked in mock surprise.

"Yes, really," Blake said calmly. If he was bothered by Greg's behaviour, he didn't show it. "In fact, I came here to advise you to go under police protection."

"Police protection?" Greg said sceptically as he crossed his arms. "Like bodyguards?"

Blake remained calm. "We can relocate you to a hotel in the next town, and keep your location hidden. You can delegate this land deal to other members of your team."

Greg gaped and moved his mouth wordlessly for a second. It didn't take him long to recover. "That's your grand plan? I go into hiding?"

Blake tapped a stack of papers on the desk. "You are the target, so it's safer for everyone if no one knows your exact location."

"Safer for everyone? Like my wife?" Greg demanded, his eyes blazing.

"Like Sibyl, Cressida, and Mr Buttons." Blake

fixed Greg with a stern. "People who are not part of your land deal. People who are involved because you had to bring work with you. People who are in the crossfire of anyone who might be aiming at you. No one else needs to be collateral damage."

"And then what?" Greg demanded, as he slammed an open palm on the table. "What happens in the next deal if they think I can be chased off? The next? A family member is targeted? An accident at my house?"

He banged his fist on the table. "I need to finish this. Here, in the open, to show them there's nothing they do can stop me, no matter how extreme!"

"Like killing your wife?" Blake glared at Greg.

"I can't protect the dead," Greg said in a quieter voice.

"But I can protect the living," Blake said at once. "And until we have a lead on why someone would try to kill you, how they knew where you would be, and when you would be there, and then managed to get to the room first, until we have this information, you and everyone here is in danger. You will be safer in a non-disclosed location."

"Out of the question," Greg snapped. "I'm not going to let them think they can chase me off this land deal."

Blake crossed his arms over his chest. "How do you know it's about the land deal?"

"What else could it be?" Greg demanded as he threw out his arms in exasperation. "It has to be someone connected to the land deal. Who else would come here?"

"Enemies, people who owe you money, blackmailers, a jealous ex, even someone who didn't approve of the wedding. The list would probably be pretty long if you stopped blustering and gave us details beyond this land deal."

"My personal life is no one's business," Greg said quickly.

"It *is* people's business. Especially when your personal life could get someone killed," Blake said levelly.

Greg shot Blake a killer glare, but Blake did not seem to care.

"I'm not going to give anyone the satisfaction of going into hiding." Greg set his jaw stubbornly. "What if I allow the police to stay here at the boarding house and accompany me? The whole building is under police protection, right? Problem solved."

Cressida stood up and waved a hand in disagreement. "Wait! No. It's bad enough that we're in the news with all that's happened. If there are police stomping around, then no one will feel comfortable staying here!"

"Do you want me to leave?" Greg demanded.

"Of course not!" Cressida shook her head. "But you need to be safe, Greg. We do worry about you. But police all over the place?"

Something in Greg's expression made me concerned. I figured that he would be a lot more rational about Blake's encouragement to relocate if he were not distracted by the death of his wife.

Blake sighed and rubbed at the bridge of his nose. "I'll see if I can get clearance for surveillance, until the deal's finalised, or the murderer is apprehended, whichever comes first."

Greg gave a thin smile. "Good. Then everyone gets what they want."

I shook my head. All I had wanted was a quiet night to catch up on my paperwork. Cressida wanted an end to the drama. Blake wanted Greg someplace else. I didn't see any winners in this argument.

CHAPTER 11

I was sitting in the private dining room that night, having been invited to dinner by Cressida. Cressida and Mr Buttons had decided that Greg would dine with them from now on, as it was not wise for him to be eating in the main dining room with the protesters around. Now, Greg was sitting at the far end of the table and staring off into space, as if he were lost in thought.

A thunderstorm was brewing, and the air almost cracked with electricity. It did nothing to lift the mood in the room, despite the fact that rain was desperately needed by the whole district.

Cressida's voice broke through the tense

atmosphere. "Please, let's just focus on having one normal night. It's been a stressful and heartbreaking week."

Greg started to cry, but he appeared to be fighting to keep himself composed. I looked at him with sympathy, but then I noticed that Mr Buttons was watching him intently. I had no idea why, but planned to find out later.

"I know we can't express how truly sorry we are for your loss, Greg, but we want to make sure that the rest of your stay here is as good as it can be," Cressida said sincerely, before signalling for everyone to eat.

I watched her glance over at Mr Buttons, acknowledging that by that point he had already started eating. Cressida didn't appear to be annoyed or upset, but it was apparent to me that everything was starting to take a toll on her.

Greg looked at his full plate, but didn't take even the smallest bite. "I'd like to say something, if I may," he began. We all nodded, and he continued. "This has been the hardest week of my life. They say you can't start to heal until you grieve the loss of a loved one, but how can you begin to grieve and try to come back from such devastation if nobody lets you?" He looked around the table. "I'm sorry. It's just so frustrating. First the cops were poking around—no offence to your friend, Sergeant Wessley," he said. "Then my car got destroyed, and then those weirdoes put on a huge protest rally, and for what? To stop my company from expanding our business? It's ridiculous. Let me mourn my wife." He paused and covered his eyes. "I just want to say goodbye to her properly, to come to terms with everything, and to find out who did this to her, if this was indeed intentional."

Everyone looked around at each other. "That's entirely understandable, Greg," Cressida said. "The police are just doing their jobs, but your poor wife, the vandalism, the council complaints, and everything else all at once is unbearable. We're here to help alleviate some of your pressure and share it."

Greg smiled and nodded.

"I know you don't hold any hard feelings against Blake personally," Mr Buttons said, "but it's important for you to understand that typical police procedure requires them by law to interview possible witnesses and suspects immediately after a crime has been committed and reported. It would be a complete travesty if your wife's killer went free and no justice was handed down."

Greg's lips trembled, but he didn't speak.

"We all just want to see justice served," Mr Buttons added.

Greg bit off a piece of meat and spoke with a full mouth. "That's all I ask." The words were mumbled and difficult to hear, but it was clear enough to keep the room silent. Greg sloshed the food around in his mouth and took a deep gulp. Mr Buttons cringed at the sight.

Greg let out a sigh before speaking again. "I don't mean to sound like a jerk at all. I'm just so heartbroken and lost right now. It's so hard to accept. The vandalism isn't really anything in the grand scheme of things, but I lost my loving wife, and now a bunch of wilderness conservationists are trying to make me lose my business, too. I just feel like I'm losing everything, and I can't do anything to stop it from happening."

We all continued in silence for some time. I knew that none of us approved of Greg destroying the wilderness area, but we weren't about to say anything about it, what with his wife so recently dying.

Dorothy swept in and cleared the plates, while shooting evil glares at Greg. I felt like shooting evil glares at Greg too, as he had just refused dessert. I had been looking forward to it, but Cressida had not mentioned it again after Greg's refusal.

"Would anyone like cards?" Mr Buttons suddenly blurted, causing everyone to jump. "How about you, Greg?"

Greg had risen half out of his seat, but he sat back down. "Err, yes," he said, but he didn't sound too willing.

With a flourish, Mr Buttons pulled a box covered with a piece of silk from his pocket. At that moment, there was a loud clap of thunder, and Greg gasped.

"We need the rain, but I hope we don't get hail," Cressida said, oblivious to Greg's jumpy demeanour. "My weather app says there's a ninety percent chance of a thunderstorm."

Mr Buttons handed Greg the deck. "Please shuffle these, and then put them back down on the table."

Greg did as he was told, until Mr Buttons took the cards back and started turning them over. "What?" Greg gasped. "I thought you wanted me to play a hand of poker or blackjack or something with you. What is this?"

Mr Buttons paid him no mind, and continued laying out the cards on the table. Then he flipped each one face up. "The moon," Mr Buttons said. "The devil. Deception exists around you. Take that how you will, but I know what I take it to mean."

Greg looked agitated. "They're just cards, man. You already tricked me into letting you read my cards or whatever they call it, but can I just catch a break for once? I just need one single night of relaxation. My mind needs it more than my body does." With that, he hurried from the room, without so much as thanking Cressida for dinner.

"Something seems off about him; that's all I'm saying," Mr Buttons said in a hushed tone.

"Mr Buttons, why do you think he's being deceptive?" I said. "Do you think he knows something he's not telling anyone, or do you just think he's aware that his work might have caused his wife's death?"

Mr Buttons frowned. "I'm not really sure what I think yet, but I believe the cards. He's lying about something. He might not even know he's lying, but there's something dishonest about that man. Have you noticed that when he cried, not a single tear could be seen?"

"Mr Buttons is right," Cressida said. "Why, Lord Farringdon told me only this morning that Greg is not to be trusted."

With that, Lord Farringdon waddled out from under the vast, starched linen tablecloth, and hissed in the direction of the door.

I stroked Lord Farringdon, and said my goodbyes to Cressida and Mr Buttons. "Thank you so much for dinner, Cressida."

"Anytime, dear. You know that." She smiled warmly. "Would you like an umbrella or a raincoat? There's an old Drizabone too, but I think it has spiders in the pockets. They might be redbacks, so if you borrow it, don't put your hands in the pockets."

I crossed to the window to look out. "No thanks, Cressida. The rain hasn't quite started yet. If I hurry, I'll get home before it does."

I made my way to the front door, and flung it open. I loved electrical storms, and particularly the time between the lightning and the rain. There was a flash of lightning, and I could see a police car parked at the front gate.

The first drops of rain were falling, and I ran down the pathway to the driver's window. Blake rolled the window down. "Would you like a police escort home?" he said.

I laughed. "Sure, why not. What are you doing here?"

Blake opened his door and got out of his car. "Maintaining a police presence at the boarding house. Has Cressida had any trouble with Greg and the protesters being under the same roof?"

I shook my head. "Not as far as I know. I think it's all okay."

We took off at a fast pace towards my cottage. "Sibyl, I'm not saying that you should change your routine, your life, or anything of the sort," Blake said. "All I'm saying is that Greg is a target. That means he has a large, red circle on his back, with possibly more than one person aiming to take him down. This wilderness protection stuff is serious, and his company refuses to compromise with the protesters in any way. He's bringing it on himself, but letting him stay here is just bringing all of the danger he's inviting onto you guys too. I care about you."

We had reached my front gate, and I turned

to Blake, but he opened my gate for me to walk through.

I opened my front door, and switched on the light. I was about to invite Blake in, but he was already heading back down the path. To make matters worse, the rain stopped abruptly.

CHAPTER 12

I put Sandy in the back yard after our morning walk, and went to the boarding house for breakfast. I headed for the private dining room, intent on asking Mr Buttons why he had not shown up for dog walking once again that morning.

Cressida was talking as I walked into the room and took my seat at the imposing mahogany dining table. "For all we know, it could be that female assistant of his who chased him around the establishment," Cressida said to Mr Buttons.

"Julie?" I asked, although I already knew the answer. "She seems a little unpleasant, but surely she isn't dangerous."

Just then, I slipped into a vision. Cressida and

Mr Buttons faded away, replaced by mist. Julie walked out of the mist, holding a box in her hands, and then Mr Buttons and Cressida appeared behind her, looking over her shoulder.

"Do you really think she could have had something to do with it?" Mr Buttons asked Cressida.

Julie shook her head, and then handed them the box. They both opened it, and then they nodded.

"Aha," Mr Buttons said to Cressida. "Julie's given us the answer."

I came to my senses, and looked around the room. Clearly, Cressida and Mr Buttons had not noticed me zoning out, or whatever I did when I was experiencing a vision, as they were still talking to each other.

"Do you really think she could have had something to do with it?" Mr Buttons asked Cressida.

His words chilled me to the bone, considering I had just experienced those very words in my vision only seconds earlier.

Cressida thought about it for a few moments. "I just saw how she was acting the other day after it all happened, and it didn't seem like she was saddened by the news in the least. Something just didn't feel right about it, but that doesn't mean she would've done something like that."

"Maybe we should talk to Greg about her," I said. "I'm sure if she's a homicidal maniac, he'd have some clue about it."

"You never know. Sometimes people are completely blind to betrayal from within," Mr Buttons said softly.

Cressida looked down at her watch. "Well, he usually comes down around this time. So, unless he's sleeping in this morning, we should be able to find a nice, subtle way to ask him about his personal assistant any time soon."

Mr Buttons and I nodded. "Hey, Mr Buttons," I said. "I missed you on our walk this morning."

Mr Buttons looked shamefaced. "Sorry. I was actually heading down to your cottage, when I saw that Dorothy had some teaspoons mixed in with some forks, so I had to rearrange all the cutlery. It took a long time, as some of the knives needed polishing."

Cressida and I shot each other a quick look, but were saved from speaking—anyway, what was there to say?—by Greg's arrival.

"Hey, what's up?" he said by way of greeting, as he poked his head around the door.

"Same old thing, just a new day. How are you holding up?" asked Mr Buttons.

"It's been rough, but I think I'm starting to accept things a bit better. Sorry about any comments I might or might not have made recently. I just have a hard time holding back my mouth when my heart's aching so badly." He frowned and pursed his lips.

"I understand, Greg," Mr Buttons said. "We're all shaken up too, with the recent events, and on top of that, the council is threatening to shut down Cressida because they say that the balcony collapsed due to faulty construction, or some such nonsense."

Greg nodded, but I noticed a light in his eyes. "I hope the inspectors aren't right. It'd be a shame if this place was actually at fault for my wife's death."

Cressida jumped to her feet. "Are you serious?" she snapped. "You know very well that balcony was one hundred percent safe."

To me, Greg looked smug rather than contrite. "I didn't mean anything by it. I'm sorry. I was just saying that it's possible. I certainly hope that isn't what happened, but it sounds like the most logical answer, unless that crazy guy who vandalised my car was in on it."

I thought I'd better say something. "Do you think your personal assistant would have any reason for trying to hurt you or your wife?"

Mr Buttons kicked me under the table. "You were supposed to say something subtle," he said in a stage whisper, a comment which would have been heard not only by Greg, but probably by half the residents of the boarding house as well.

Greg frowned and appeared to be thinking about what to say. "Julie?" he said, as he walked into the room. "She definitely would have had a reason to hurt either one of us. She hits on me all the time. That woman has been trying to have an affair with me for a long time, even when Lisa was still alive!"

"Have you had an affair with her?" Mr Buttons said.

"Mr Buttons!" Cressida and I exclaimed in unison.

Greg's hands flew to his throat. "No, I would never cheat on my wife," he said loudly, fixing Mr Buttons with a glare. "That woman has just always had a thing for me. Every time I tell her no, she gets all crazy and makes being around her miserable. I don't know if she would ever go so far as to hurt anyone, though. I didn't even consider her a suspect before now," he added.

Greg crossed to a window and stared out. "Maybe I should just fire her," he said quietly. "Even if she didn't hurt Lisa, if it gets out that she's been hitting on me and I allowed it to continue, I'll be made a fool in the public's eyes. I'm going to have a talk with her." With that, he hurried to the door, and closed it quietly behind him.

Cressida sighed. "There are better ways to start a morning."

"I think I'm going to pay Blake a visit," I said. "I don't know if he's even looked into the personal assistant's history. He should at least be made aware of her, and the fact that she's shown interest in the victim's husband."

Mr Buttons nodded. "Okay, but can't you just call him?"

Cressida elbowed him. "You silly man."

Mr Buttons' cheeks flushed. "Oh, sorry."

I could feel my cheeks flush, too. I said my goodbyes and hurried to my van.

I was a little embarrassed, but, truth be told, I

was looking forward to seeing Blake. It was funny that he had just left me on my doorstep like that, and I wondered if anything was wrong.

As I pulled over outside the police station, I smiled. The thought of seeing Blake again always filled me with excitement.

I opened the door with anticipation, but then stopped in surprise. Blake was standing behind the front desk with a young, attractive woman. The two were talking like best friends. I caught my breath and turned to leave, but before I reached the door, Blake called me back.

"Sibyl, this is Rachel Winters. Rachel, this is Sibyl Potts."

The two of us shook hands. Blake did not introduce the woman as his girlfriend, thankfully, but neither did he give any clue as to her identity.

Rachel left, after waving to Blake flirtatiously, or so it seemed to me.

Blake must have caught my expression, as he hurried to explain. "Rachel's an old friend," he said. "She's one of the protesters. She's back in town for the protest rallies."

I nodded. I was more than a little jealous, to be honest. I took a deep breath. "Well, I'm here about Julie, Greg's personal assistant. Greg told us that she's been trying to start up some sort of affair with him for quite a while now."

"Does he think she wanted to hurt him, or Lisa?"

I shrugged. "He isn't sure, but maybe Julie thought he'd be all hers if the wife was removed from the picture."

"Thanks, Sibyl. I'll look into it."

I nodded, and made to leave, but Blake caught my arm. "Sibyl," he began, but then Constable Andrews burst through the door, and hurried to the front office.

Blake abruptly released my arm. "That was my ex-girlfriend."

"Ex-girlfriend?" I parroted.

Blake nodded. "Yes, Rachel Winters is my ex-girlfriend." He stressed the ex.

It was my turn to nod. Rachel Winters, the New Agey type, as the townspeople had described her. Was she really in town for the protest rallies, or did she have another agenda, an agenda that involved Blake?

CHAPTER 13

I was walking down the main street with Mr Buttons and Cressida. We were on our way to Nathan's Hardware Store. Cressida was determined to fill some tiny cracks in the plaster walls, as she was sure that the council would condemn the building if they saw them. Mr Buttons and I had assured her that all old buildings have hairline cracks here and there, but our assurances had fallen on deaf ears.

Mr Buttons was still convinced that Dorothy was the one responsible for Lisa's death. "That awful woman, Dorothy, is the murderer. I'm sure of it," he said for what seemed to me like the millionth time. "She has a frightful temper. She and Lisa did have a terrible argument, and, as far as I can see, that's the end of the matter. Problem solved."

Cressida shook her head. "Do you really think Dorothy would actually kill someone for complaining about her cooking?" she asked.

"You never know," Mr Buttons insisted. "She has a bad temper. I just think the wife was the intended victim, and that Dorothy was somehow involved. Besides, her eyebrows are crooked."

Cressida and I exchanged glances.

A thought occurred to me. "How could the wife have been the intended victim?"

"What?" Cressida asked me. "What does that have to do with eyebrows?"

"Nothing," I said. "Mr Buttons, you said that you think Lisa was the intended victim."

Mr Buttons nodded.

"Greg said he always smoked out on the balcony," I said. "Lisa was hardly ever out there, so why would Dorothy, or anyone else for that matter, try to kill Lisa on the balcony if they wanted to make it look like an accident?"

Mr Buttons paused and thought about it for a while. "I guess you might have me there, but who knows?" he finally said. "Maybe Dorothy overheard Greg telling his wife he was going to smoke outside that day."

Cressida arrived at the checkout with a basket full of items. Mr Buttons walked up behind her and greeted the store's owner, who was slumped over the register. "Hi Nathan, how are you?"

The elderly, stooped man looked up and squinted at Mr Buttons. "Is that you, Mr Buttons? I've misplaced my glasses. What with the death of that poor woman, and all those people dancing around with signs and yelling about saving the wilderness area, the world's gone mad. It's a good cause, mind you, but protesting in the main street won't help them."

"It *is* a good cause," Mr Buttons said. "I'm sure if something came my way that I felt strongly about, even I would hold up a sign for a few hours to show my support. Can't blame them for trying to save the wilderness area, can you?"

I nodded. "It's an absolute crime that Greg's encroaching on the wilderness area. I wish the protests could help, but it's obvious that Greg isn't going to stop his land expansion."

"Greg?" Nathan said. "Is he doing renovations at the boarding house?"

Cressida frowned. "No," she said. "Why do you ask?"

"Oh, no reason, really. Sibyl mentioned his name, and I just then remembered him coming in here the other day." Nathan scratched his nearly bald head. "Strange thing, but old age is a fickle beast." He chuckled.

"What did Greg come here for?" Cressida asked.

"I think he bought a big wrench," Nathan said.

Cressida, Mr Buttons, and I exchanged glances. Mr Buttons wriggled his eyebrows at us. I looked back at Nathan, but he was staring in a mirror, trying to rearrange his combover.

As we were walking towards the front door of the hardware store, Mr Buttons stopped and looked up at the ceiling, and then pointed upward. "Hey, Nathan," he said, turning back to the elderly man, "is that a CCTV system?"

Nathan looked up from the mirror, and set his comb on the nearest bench. "Yes, it is. Why?"

"Do you think we could take a look at your footage for the week leading up to the recent death at the boarding house?"

Nathan looked confused. "You really should

leave that up to the police, Mr Buttons," he warned him. "Why, back in my day…"

Mr Buttons cut him off. "Oh, yes, of course we'll turn over anything we find right away. I just have a hunch about the whole thing, and if you have recordings of everyone, we can at least narrow it down to a few people who could be involved."

"You're looking for what, exactly?" Cressida asked him.

Mr Buttons looked smug. "If a certain person purchased a wrench or similar tool, she could've tinkered with the railing that collapsed." He turned back to Nathan, but he had already fallen asleep on the counter and was snoring softly.

We walked down the street to the nearest café. Mr Buttons stopped outside the entrance. "I'm still saying that Dorothy did it."

Cressida groaned. "Of course you are, Mr Buttons."

"Look, just think about this," I said. "Why would Dorothy sabotage the railing of a balcony that Greg always used? I'd think the perpetrator would have to be either someone going after Greg, like the wilderness protesters, or Greg himself going after his wife."

"How do you figure?" Mr Buttons asked in disbelief. "Why would Greg kill his own wife?"

"I don't know what the motive could be, but maybe it has to do with his assistant. Nathan said Greg bought a big wrench!"

Mr Buttons shook his head. "We know that Greg turned down his assistant, though, so I really doubt that. There's also the fact that Greg and Lisa just got married, so it's unlikely that he was already having an affair. Why would he get married in that case? It makes no sense. Plus, he's already a very wealthy man, so it's not like he did it for insurance money or something. I just don't see it." Mr Buttons shook his head again.

I walked inside the building, the tempting fragrance of coffee luring me in. "I'm just saying that Greg had an opportunity, much more so than anyone else could have. It's his room, and he used that balcony frequently. I just think it would be far less obvious to the random person walking outside if Greg was undoing some bolts, as opposed to someone like Dorothy standing up there doing it."

"You could have a point there, Sibyl," Cressida said. "And why wasn't Greg up there that day? Seems odd to me that he wanted to smoke in the yard that one time."

"Exactly," I said. "I think we might be onto something."

"But then he would have had to lure his wife onto the balcony in his place," Mr Buttons said. "Wouldn't that have been tough, too? And again, what is his motive?"

We had taken our seats at the front table, by the big window overlooking the highway. "Just because we don't know his motive doesn't mean he doesn't have one," I said. "It's possible that he called her out onto the balcony from out in the yard. She walked out, and leant over the rail, and *crash*!"

Cressida looked impressed, but Mr Buttons seemed unmoved by my theory. "It's possible, but I don't know. I still just don't buy it. Not unless you can give me a believable reason as to why a newly married man with buckets of money, a highly successful business, and everything he could possibly ask for, would risk it all away to kill the woman he had only just married."

"Who knows?" said Cressida.

"Why else smoke outside instead of on the balcony though, that one day?" I said. "Surely that's the pivotal question. We need to figure out if Greg was the actual target, or whether Lisa was the target."

Cressida and Mr Buttons looked at me. "How do we figure that out?" Mr Buttons asked.

I shrugged. "I don't have a clue."

CHAPTER 14

I was sitting in the main dining room with Cressida and Mr Buttons. The three of us were sipping our English Breakfast tea and nibbling cucumber sandwiches, perfectly cut into triangles.

Greg sat with us, but he was spending more time looking at his cup and playing with it than actually drinking from it. He slowly spun the cup around and around as it perched atop the table, stirring it with a spoon every once in a while.

"I'll have to go back to Nathan's Hardware for a trowel," Cressida said out of nowhere.

Greg looked up from his tea cup. "Nathan's Hardware?" he said. "If you ever need any supplies, I'd be happy to pick them up for you. Have you been there lately?"

I wondered why Greg was so focused on the hardware store all of a sudden. *What's he trying to hide?* I wondered. *The fact that he had bought a wrench?*

"Yes," Cressida said.

Greg simply nodded, before returning to stirring his cup.

"So, Greg, how's everything going with the wilderness area and all that?" Mr Buttons asked.

The man continued spinning his cup of tea and tuning out the world. Eventually, he looked up at Mr Buttons and spoke slowly. "It's been okay. We're still dealing with those wilderness nuts, though. On a daily basis, it seems." His tone held more than a hint of irritation.

I was annoyed. I most certainly was opposed to his destruction of the wilderness area, but I could hardly say anything. After all, he was Cressida's paying guest, and his wife had just died.

"Things will get better," Cressida said. "Sometimes I can't believe we're still standing after everything we've been through. You just have to have hope, and trust that things will work out how they are supposed to. Whoever caused your wife's demise will be punished. I know it."

THE PRAWN IDENTITY

Greg rolled his eyes, a gesture I considered to be quite rude after Cressida's kind words. He raised his cup and took a brief sip. He licked his upper lip and placed the cup down a little too hard. "I should probably head out soon. This construction site is monstrous, difficult, and full of protesters, so I might need an early start this morning."

Just as he stood to his feet, Blake and Constable Andrews walked in.

"Good morning, everyone," Blake said.

"What brings you here so early, Blake?" Cressida asked.

"I came by to see if Greg would mind accompanying us back to the station. We would like to discuss a few things about his wife's murder case with him."

Greg frowned and crossed his arms over his chest. "Will this take long?" he snapped. "I've been dragging my feet on the ground long enough because of this mess. I have work I need to get done so I can get back home and away from this circus."

"It won't take long," Blake said.

Greg shot him a dirty look, but rose from his chair and followed the officers out.

After they left, the three of us sat in silence for a few minutes.

"That was unexpected," Mr Buttons said.

Cressida nodded hard. "I thought they were arresting him at first."

I agreed. "I thought so, too," I said. "I wonder what they have to talk to him about, though. New evidence, maybe?"

"I'm confused," Mr Buttons said. "Maybe they found something that points in his direction."

Cressida chuckled. "If that's true, your Dorothy theory is out the window."

"Perhaps we should do some research," I said, to forestall another tirade by Mr Buttons as to Dorothy's likelihood as a suspect.

"Like what?" asked Cressida. "Do you mean online?"

I bit my lip. "I meant that we should look up the wife's past. If she was the intended murder victim, then we need to find out if she had any enemies."

"Good idea, Sibyl." Mr Buttons nodded. "Perhaps Lisa knew Dorothy a long time ago. We might uncover a motive for Dorothy."

"Or perhaps we'll find out why Greg would want to hurt Lisa," Cressida added.

I shook my head. "Greg seems the obvious suspect, except for one important thing. There's no motive."

"I'll get my laptop." With that, Mr Buttons left the room, leaving us to consume cucumber sandwiches and lukewarm tea.

Mr Buttons soon returned with his laptop. He booted it up, and Cressida and I looked over his shoulder.

"Hmm," Mr Buttons said. "It seems to suggest that Lisa is actually just as wealthy as Greg is. So, that rules out money as a motive, and he has plenty of it himself, doesn't he?"

I nodded. "Yes," I said. I was already bored. I was sure we wouldn't turn up anything of use.

"Well, this is odd," Mr Buttons remarked, after what seemed an age.

"What?" I said, looking at Cressida, who seemed to have zoned out, too.

"Barbara and James Madison, Lisa's parents. Hmm, now that's interesting."

"And?" Cressida prompted.

Mr Buttons paused to dab at a spot on the screen with his handkerchief. "Okay, it looks like the Madisons are in business with Greg's parents.

They're in Europe. Oh yes, Greg said that's why the funeral was delayed. Hmm."

"Why is that interesting?" Cressida asked. I was thinking the same thing.

Mr Buttons did not reply. He was diligently at work scrolling through countless URLs. I was thinking up an excuse to leave when Mr Buttons leant over and peered at the screen. "Lisa had a will."

"Okay, here it is. Hold on." Mr Buttons stared at the screen, his eyes darting left and right over and over. "Oh no, it wasn't anything."

"So basically, we're back where we started?" Cressida said, in a strained voice.

Mr Buttons nodded. "Looks like it."

"Okay, so let's go over what we know and what we don't," I said. "We know that Greg is very wealthy. We also know now that Lisa was wealthy too, before the marriage. So, I think it's safe to say that the money motive just doesn't fit into this puzzle."

"And they were only married for a short time," Mr Buttons said. "Why even marry Lisa in the first place if he didn't want to? Sure, people change their minds and want a divorce, but not days after the wedding."

"Wait," I said. "What if he didn't want to get married at all? If their parents are good friends and business partners, wouldn't it make sense that the marriage was arranged?"

Mr Buttons looked at me strangely. "Who in Australia has an arranged marriage? I really don't think their marriage was arranged, and even if it was, I think saying no is a much better tool to get out of it than murder."

"You never know with those high society types though," Cressida said.

I sighed. "I didn't mean an arranged marriage as such. I meant that their parents might've put pressure on both of them. Perhaps it was expected of them both from an early age and they just fell into it." I sighed again. "Really, I don't have a clue. You know what they say, money and love are the usual motives for murder, and I can't see how Lisa's murder fits either."

Cressida sighed. "We're back where we started from." Mr Buttons agreed, and then took his coins out of his wallet and polished them.

CHAPTER 15

Mr Buttons, Cressida, and I arrived in Little Tatterford, heading for the first of the many cafés that dotted the main street.

"And what will you ladies have for lunch today? My treat, of course," Mr Buttons said, as he held open the door for us to enter.

"You don't have to do that, Mr Buttons," I responded, earning me a waved hand in response.

"I insist." Mr Buttons' tone was no-nonsense.

"Well then, if you insist," Cressida said, nudging me to go along with it. "Thank you. I do appreciate it."

I smiled. "Thank you, Mr Buttons."

We took our usual table at the front of the

café. Cressida and I looked at the menus, while Mr Buttons repositioned the menus throughout the café in the centre of the tables.

"What will you ladies have?" he asked, upon his return to our table.

"I'll have my usual, the macadamia apple crusted pork loin, please," Cressida said.

Mr Buttons furrowed his brow at Cressida. "Macadamia nuts give you heartburn."

"Yes, but it's worth it," Cressida sighed contently. "It's just too delicious."

"Did you take your medication?"

"No, I forgot on the way out."

"Well then, take one now," Mr Buttons insisted.

"Then I would have to wait thirty minutes to eat." Cressida shook her head stubbornly. "I don't want to wait."

Mr Buttons looked up from rearranging the lilies on the table. "Cressida, waiting a few minutes won't kill you. You'll swear at those macadamia nuts in an hour, though," Mr Buttons fussed at her.

I smiled as a light bickering session started up between them. Things were so normal today. It was such a refreshing change of pace compared to what we had been dealing with lately. I decided to have the bruschetta laden with sundried tomatoes, olives, basil, and parmesan cheese, and so turned my attention from the menu to the room.

As I did so, my stomach dropped.

Blake was sitting at a table. His back was to me, but I'd know him anywhere. He had not turned around to say hello to us, so I guessed he hadn't even seen us come in. He seemed completely fixated on the person he was talking to, his ex-girlfriend, the gorgeous Rachel Winters.

They seemed comfortable together. Rachel was laughing, and Blake appeared to be hanging on her every word.

I tried not to feel the sharp pangs of hurt as I watched them chatter away like they were in their own little world. I couldn't see Blake's expression, but he seemed to be having a lovely time.

I was in the depths of despair. *Maybe there's a reason we never went out for a second dinner*, I thought.

"Earth to Sibyl," Cressida said, startling me back to the moment.

"Did you know what you wanted?" Mr Buttons asked.

"Oh yes, the bruschetta laden with sundried tomatoes, olives, basil, and parmesan, please." I forced a smile, and did my best not to allow the unexpected scene to throw me off my lunch. It was my fault that I'd assumed that Blake had been interested in me. I didn't have a right to pout and turn our lunch into a soap opera.

"Is everything all right?" Cressida asked with concern, following my gaze. She looked surprised as she spied Blake and the woman. "Oh, don't worry about any of that. That's just his ex. It's nothing to worry about."

"They broke off on friendly terms." Mr Buttons gave me a smile of reassurance. "They figured out they were no good for each other, but managed to salvage a good friendship after the relationship went south."

Cressida studied my face. "They're just friends," she insisted. "Whatever reason they met up, I'm sure it's no big deal. How about we go over and say hi?"

"No, no, no!" I exclaimed. "That's okay." I shook my head. "You're right. It's probably nothing."

I wished I believed my own words. It wasn't my business who Blake saw, or why. I didn't want to become that obsessed stalker with too many cats, or in my case, a dog and a trash-talking cockatoo.

I just wished I had not let myself think we had been building more than a friendship. I glanced back at the pair. My ex-husband, Andrew, had been friendly with many women, a lot friendlier than I had realised at the time. I'd stupidly trusted in our relationship, and that blind trust had nearly gotten me killed.

Oh, stop it, I silently rebuked myself. Blake wasn't anything like that man. It was my own fault for making assumptions about an imaginary chemistry between us.

"Are sure you're okay, Sibyl?" Cressida asked with concern.

"I'm okay. It'll all be fine," I said, as I waved my hand gently. "It just threw me off. It's all good," I lied.

Cressida persisted. "They really are just friends."

"I'm happy they were able to stay friends," I said quickly. It truly wasn't any of my business. The last thing I wanted to do was get my friends worried about me, especially when friendship was probably all Blake and I would have as well. I thought back on the times when he'd rushed to my rescue. He'd looked so angry when I'd been arrested by mistake. He'd always gone out of his way to see if I was okay.

In hindsight, that's what friends do. I was sure Blake would have done the same for Mr Buttons or Cressida. It was just how he was. It was my own imagination fooling me into thinking it was turning into more than that.

"Our food will be out in about fifteen minutes," Mr Buttons said, as he returned to his seat after ordering. He shot Cressida a pleading look. "Cressida, for all that is good and right in the world, take something before you eat those macadamia nuts. You'll love it so much less by dinner. I beg you to take appropriate measures."

Cressida sighed dramatically and dug through her bag for the pills for her heartburn, which had been flaring up quite a lot lately with all the stress. "All right. But only because you are begging."

Mr Buttons grinned at her. "I could beg on my knee if it will make you take it that much faster."

Cressida laughed. "Go for it." Her eyes widened in alarm as he rose and started to drop to the floor, snagging his sleeve. "I was kidding. Kidding. I'm taking it right now, look."

"Are you sure?" Mr Buttons asked, a mischievous glint in his eye. "I could sing my concerns for you if you like."

"I'm taking the medicine—just don't make a scene." Cressida laughed nervously as she brandished her heartburn pills. "You're tone deaf anyway."

I found myself muffling a laugh as Mr Buttons climbed back into his chair, looking pleased that he had taken Cressida by surprise. I loved these two. They always had a way of making me feel better by just being themselves.

"While we wait on our meals, shall we try to solve the mystery of Lisa's death?" Mr Buttons asked, as he leant back, conveniently blocking my view of Blake's table.

That sounded fine to me; I could do with a distraction. I'd sort out my heart and head later in a less public place, preferably over some salted caramel ice cream and a rerun of *Monty Python* or *The Young Ones*. I could do with some classic silliness.

"It had to be Greg," Cressida said, after she took a sip of her soda to wash down the medicine. "I'm betting his new bride had a really nice life insurance policy."

"Oh come now. You've seen how broken up he is over the whole thing," Mr Buttons pointed out. "Besides, if insurance was his motive, he would've waited until they had been married for much longer than a day or two."

Cressida looked sceptical. "Money does weird things to people. He didn't take time off his work to mourn."

"People deal with grief differently," Mr Buttons said. "He might be burying himself in his work."

I bit a fingernail. "Who else would have known Greg's room number? Or been able to get into the room with no one noticing?" I asked. I had to side with Cressida on this one. Greg's behaviour was indeed strange, even for someone in mourning. He didn't act like he had lost the love of his life when he was making land deals and chasing off protesters.

"My money is on our dear Dorothy." Mr Buttons grimaced as he brought up the woman's name. "She knew Greg's room number, of course. It would've been easy to go up there wielding a wrench. She's a few kangaroos short of a herd."

"Why would she do that, though?" Cressida asked, unconvinced. "I know you don't like her,

Mr Buttons. But really, we can't accuse someone just because she's unlikeable."

"How much do we really know about her, though?" Mr Buttons asked. "Look at that time when the ghost hunters came to town. None of us saw her connection there, until it slapped us in the face."

"And Dorothy was also on the suspect list then," I said. "We can't throw her on the list every time we get stumped by something."

"We can if she's a mean woman who has the access and ability to do it," Mr Buttons countered.

Cressida raised her eyebrows. "But again, why would she do it? We don't have any way to connect her to Greg. The only motive is her big fight with Lisa the night before the murder."

I shrugged. "I suppose it's possible that she's related to one of the protesters, but that's quite a stretch."

"Greg is the one with the motive," Cressida said. "His whole life involves the bottom line. Most of his opponents backed off out of respect for the loss of his wife, too. Maybe she was worth more to him dead than alive."

"That's a pretty grim picture to paint," Mr Buttons said doubtfully. "Killing his wife for sympathy? That's the most tenuous motive I've ever heard."

"Hi, Cressida and Mr Buttons," a feminine voice said, interrupting our debate.

To my horror, I turned my head to see an unhappy Blake and his overly cheerful and pretty ex-girlfriend standing by our table. "It's been forever. How have you both been?"

Blake gave an awkward greeting. I tried to push down a wave of anxiety as Blake avoided my gaze. It wasn't like I was following him or anything. He didn't have to act upset I was there.

"Hi Blake," I said, in an even tone.

Rachel stuck out her hand to shake mine. "Hi again, Sibyl."

I mumbled a polite greeting as I shook the woman's hand. Blake did not look at all pleased that the two of us were speaking. Unpleasant memories of my ex-husband flooded back. I reminded myself once more that Blake was nothing like him.

"Sorry, I have to get to a meeting, but I'll leave you all to talk. Be good, Blake. Don't do anything I wouldn't do." The woman winked and waved to Cressida and Mr Buttons, before making a rush out the door.

Blake shot me an apologetic look. Well, I thought it was apologetic. I didn't know what he had to apologise to me about. Nothing changed the fact that we were only friends, and not a couple.

At least things couldn't get any worse.

CHAPTER 16

Mr Buttons and I had been googling for hours, or at least it sure felt like it had been that long.

"So, what else do you want to look up?" Mr Buttons asked me.

I was mentally exhausted. I couldn't think of a single avenue that we had not pursued.

"Top ten men who murdered their wives," Cressida interjected from her position behind the table. She shuffled her paperwork for a moment. "He might not be on those lists yet, but perhaps his motive is," she added, before returning to her work.

I laughed, but I knew she might be right. "Go for it," I said to Mr Buttons. "Let's see if there are any cases of men who murdered their wives for unusual motives."

We got back to work sifting through the mountains of links.

"What about this one then?" Mr Buttons asked, stabbing his finger at the screen. "This man killed his wife because she was going to turn him in for embezzling company funds."

Cressida walked over and stuck her face towards the screen. "Hmm, something like that would definitely make sense," she said. The three of us peered at the screen. Moments later, the door swung open and Greg strolled in, looking distraught.

Mr Buttons slammed the laptop shut.

"Hello, everyone," Greg said, his face pinched and white. His hands went to his face.

"We were just seeing what the weather was going to look like for the week," Cressida said. "That thunderstorm didn't bring much rain." She wasn't a good liar, but Greg did not appear to notice.

"Thanks," he said as he sat down. "The police held me for hours and hours, asking me the very same things over and over again. It's all been so overwhelming and intense. Days after I lose my wife, and I'm dealing with all of this craziness. I'm about to lose my mind."

"What did they ask you?" Mr Buttons said.

"They just kept grilling me about times. What time did I shower that day? What time did I eat? When was the last time I saw Lisa that morning? Just a bunch of those types of things. Oh, and the one thing they really harped on about was a wrench."

"A wrench?" Mr Buttons asked.

"Apparently a man at that hardware store in town told some people that I was in his store a few days before my wife passed away. The police accused me of buying the wrench used to disable the railing, which ultimately killed Lisa." He looked into his empty hands and sniffled. "I didn't hurt my wife. I loved her and I miss her very much."

I wasn't sure what to believe, and by the look Cressida was giving me, I felt we were on the same page. I glanced over at Mr Buttons and noticed he looked more sympathetic. He probably still thought Dorothy was the murderer. I shook my head at the idea.

Greg pulled his head from his palms and

looked up. "It was just really exhausting, but at least it's all cleared up."

"What?" the three of us asked at once.

Greg fixed me with a look that I was sure was smug. "The police looked at the CCTV footage from the hardware store. They traced the buyer of a wrench back to a man named Alex Jefferson. He's a tad older, but to an elderly man like the hardware store owner, he and I looked like twins."

"A good thing they caught their mistake before it was too late or something. You poor man," Mr Buttons said, with genuine feeling.

Greg nodded vehemently. "Yes, that's the only thing that made them let me go home. Once they found out it wasn't me, they had nothing to hold me on. They still went over a few questions and oddities in the case, but from how they were treating me near the end and such, I feel confident they'll be looking for the actual killer now, instead of wasting their time barking up the wrong trees." Greg slammed a clenched fist onto the table in front of him. "I just want to finish this expansion, have the case closed and solved, and get on with my life. Me being here right now is not good for any of us." Greg shot me a look when he said that, and for some reason, I felt it was a threat.

"I'm going to go rest for a bit and then get back to work," Greg said. He nodded to us and then left.

Cressida shook her head. "Can you believe that?"

"What?" Mr Buttons said.

"Was Nathan wrong? It wasn't even Greg? He seemed so sure," I said. "Anyway, just as well you handed the footage straight over to the police, Mr Buttons."

We all fell silent as Greg poked his head back around the door.

"Oh, one more thing," Greg said. "Have any of you seen a pair of black, high heel pumps? The designer is Burch. They were Lisa's favourite formal shoes, but I can't find them anywhere, and I know she brought them for our honeymoon."

"Oh, that's the first I've heard of any missing items. I'll ask the staff if they've found any shoes," Cressida said.

Greg thanked her and disappeared.

"It's kind of weird that he'd even be looking for his wife's shoes, isn't it?" Mr Buttons asked.

"Not if he just wants to make sure he doesn't lose anything of hers he has left," I said.

Cressida left the room in search of the missing shoes, while Mr Buttons and I went back to googling motives for murder.

"Would you believe it?"

I jumped and looked back at Cressida. I hadn't heard her return to the room. "Lisa's shoes were sitting right in the Lost and Found bin. Someone turned them in yesterday, but the log wasn't filled out properly. It just says, 'Kitchen staff,'" Cressida said.

"How would kitchen staff find shoes missing from a guest's room?" I asked.

Cressida shrugged.

"I was right!" Mr Buttons exclaimed. "It was Dorothy! She's the only kitchen staff we have."

"What are you talking about? You think Dorothy stole Lisa's shoes?" I asked him.

Mr Buttons was unable to hide his enthusiasm. "It fits," he said gleefully. "Maybe that was why the poor woman went out on the balcony. She probably wanted to ask Greg, whom she knew was outside in the yard smoking, if he knew where they were."

I thought about it for a moment. "Well, that

makes sense, but still, I really can't believe it was Dorothy who took the shoes, let alone hurt Lisa."

Cressida stood up. "I'll speak with her about it."

"What? You're just going to walk up to Dorothy and ask her about it?" I asked.

"Yes, why not? If she did, the police will want to be made aware of it." Cressida hurried off, and I hurried after her.

We were met at the kitchen door by the grumpy woman. "What is it? I'm behind as it is!"

Cressida stepped forward. "Dorothy, I'm here about an important matter. A pair of shoes went missing from a guest, and the entry says they were turned into Lost and Found by kitchen staff. You're the only kitchen staff here. We need to know who found the shoes."

"What does it matter?" Dorothy snapped.

"The shoes belong to the guest who died. The police are investigating it as a homicide, so they will want to know how someone came to have the woman's possessions, and why," Cressida said sternly.

Dorothy frowned, and crossed her arms over her chest. "I know it looks bad, but that's why I turned them in. That argument I had with her the night before. I know people are thinking I did something to harm her because I was angry, but I didn't."

"Dorothy, you have a history of losing your temper with guests," Cressida said.

Dorothy narrowed her eyes, but her tone was even. "I did lose my temper, but not enough to kill someone. I stole the shoes because I was going to line them with some small slices of fish, so they'd stink the next time she wore them. Then, she ended up getting murdered. I cleaned the shoes and then threw them in the Lost and Found, hoping they'd be returned and nobody would ask questions."

CHAPTER 17

I had a break between grooming clients, so I wandered up to the boarding house to see if there had been any developments.

Cressida was sitting on the front steps, her head in her hands. "The Little Tatterford and Shire Council is sending an inspector here today." She sighed and rolled her eyes at the thought.

"Why would they?" I said. "The police are treating Lisa's death as suspicious."

Cressida sighed and looked away. "I don't know, but I don't think it's a good thing. It's like someone at that place has a grudge against me."

"Unless that awful Cynthia Devonshire from the B&B in town has a friend who works for the council, I honestly don't think she'd have that kind of influence."

Cressida frowned. It was clear that she was overwhelmed with anxiety. "You never know, Cynthia Devonshire could be more powerful than we realise. Have you spoken to Blake recently?"

"No," I said, my heart sinking. "Not since the other day. Why?"

"Oh, just wondering," Cressida replied. "I was wondering if you thought I should notify the police about the shoes that went missing."

That caught me off guard completely. "I don't know. What do you think?"

Cressida's face contorted, and the makeup around her eyes cracked. "I don't really think it pertains to the case at all."

"You and I think that, but what if we're wrong?"

Cressida wrung her hands. "But then Dorothy will become a suspect." She shrugged. "At least that would make Mr Buttons happy."

I thought for a while. "I suppose we need to do what's right," I said.

Cressida's face softened. "Yes, that makes sense," she said.

Mr Buttons hurried over to us. "What are you two talking about?"

"Sibyl and I were discussing whether or not to inform the police about Dorothy stealing the shoes, and we came to the conclusion that we should tell them," Cressida said.

Mr Buttons nodded. "Yes, the police need to know that she hid her theft from them," he said. "It shows that she's deceitful."

I was waiting for Cressida to disagree, when a white truck pulled up suddenly, spraying gravel everywhere. Cressida stopped mid-sentence and looked panicked when Franklin Greer climbed out of the car.

"Good afternoon, Ms Upthorpe," he said. "We've met before. As you know, my name is Franklin Greer, and I'm from the Little Tatterford and Shire Council. I'm here to inspect some of the key features of this establishment. I'm going to let you in on one little secret." He smiled a thin smile.

The man stood wordlessly for some length of time, so Cressida finally broke the silence. "What's the secret?"

Franklin Greer smiled in an evil manner. He reminded me of a villain from a comic book. He turned his head and spoke in a low voice. "We have some inside information that this boarding house is not operating under the correct procedural and structural guidelines and standards. Failure to comply with any of our requests, whether they be for information, documents, customer and guest information, or anything of the sort that we deem necessary, will lead to the temporary closure of this establishment for an indefinite period of time, or until the issue is resolved in a satisfactory manner set forth by the Little Tatterford and Shire Council."

"Yes," Cressida finally said. Her voice was filled with fear and concern. "Give me a few moments to make sure that the guests vacate their rooms for your inspection."

"That won't be necessary," Franklin Greer said, his smirk spreading. "I'm stopping all operations of this establishment at this time. All guests will need to vacate their rooms until further notice. We will not evict you, the owner, or your family, but that is all we'll allow here until the business license is restored. That will happen upon one of two things, when a complete and lengthy inspection reveals no proof or signs of structural or procedural violations, or when violations are discovered, but fines and repairs are made by the offender as ordered by the Little Tatterford and Shire Council." He smiled in a smug, threatening way. "I believe that means you will be one of the guests vacating your room," he said, looking at me.

I resisted the urge to stomp on his foot. "Actually, I live in the cottage out back. I don't board here, so I get to stay, too," I said.

Franklin Greer ignored me. "Excuse me, sir," he said to Mr Buttons.

Mr Buttons glared at him. "Yes?"

"Are you a guest here?"

Mr Buttons looked like a kangaroo in the headlights, frozen and unsure of what to do. I wondered if time was at a stand-still in his mind, while little gears spun around, trying to come up with the right solution to his quandary.

Cressida moved to position herself between Franklin Greer and Mr Buttons. "What are you talking about?" she said. "Mr Buttons is my boyfriend. He lives with me," she said, defiantly.

I was surprised that Franklin Greer fell for such a blatant lie, but he did. His face fell with disappointment, but then soon lighted up when one of the young environmentalists hurried out the front door.

"Who is that?" he asked Cressida.

"He's Peter Steele, one of our guests," Cressida said, honestly. "There are others."

"All right, thank you for your cooperation." He smiled in a sadistic way as he approached the guest. The young man then went back into the boarding house.

Franklin Greer walked back to us. "I will inform all the guests that they will no longer be able to reside at this establishment. They are going to be packing up and vacating within a few hours."

"You can't be serious!" Cressida's voice was a wail. "Where will they go with no notice?"

"To the new Bed and Breakfast that's just opened up in town. You know of it, don't you?"

"Yes, I'm well aware," Cressida growled. "You're kicking out my guests and sending them to my biggest competitor?"

"I'm sorry, but that's our policy." He did not sound at all sorry.

Cressida's sadness turned to anger. "You can't close the boarding house before the investigation!"

THE PRAWN IDENTITY

"I apologise for the inconvenience," Franklin Greer said, as he turned away.

Cressida walked after him. "The police are investigating it as a homicide," she said to his back.

Franklin Greer stopped walking, and turned back to Cressida. "I understand that, but until we investigate the integrity of the building and see that proper protocols are being followed, it's a risk we can't take. Please evacuate your guests and allow us to conduct our inspection." He smiled, looking like a spoiled kid who just stolen a second dessert when no one was looking. "Oh, I see there's at least one more guest down here."

Greg had just appeared. "Hey guys, what's up?" he said, as he walked over to us.

Franklin Greer squinted at him. "Good afternoon. My name is Franklin Greer. I'm from the Little Tatterford and Shire Council. We're here investigating some possible issues with the building. If you're a guest, we need to ask that you leave the premises as soon as possible, for safety reasons. That is, unless you are a member of Ms Upthorpe's family. Are you?"

"No," Greg said. He was clearly unsure of how to respond to the situation.

"Mr Greer, Greg is a close friend of mine," Cressida said.

I watched Greg's eyes flicker as he caught on to what was happening. "Yes, I'm just in town briefly and needed a place to stay. Cressida and I go way back and she allowed me to stay in a room as a family guest. I haven't paid her a cent."

"That means he's not a customer or guest under business policy," Cressida elaborated.

Franklin Greer tilted his head upwards. "All right. I think we're going to schedule a thorough inspection very soon. I'll call you later with the exact time and date."

"I thought you were going to do that right now?"

"No, we need to look over a few things and give those guests time to vacate the rooms. We will be in touch."

CHAPTER 18

I clipped the leash onto Sandy's collar, and stepped outside to see Mr Buttons walking to my front door, holding Tiny, Blake's Chihuahua.

"What are you doing with Tiny?" I blurted out.

"I was just on my way down here to walk Sandy with you, when Blake drove up. He said he was on his way to see if you'd walk Tiny today," he said, "but he saw me, so he gave me Tiny and took off. He wants us to mind him for the day. He said he was in a hurry."

More like in a hurry to avoid me, I thought. Blake had sure been acting strange lately. He was probably overjoyed to see Mr Buttons and thus avoid having to ask me to walk Tiny. I shrugged. "Oh well, we might as well walk at the dog park today. Can you hold Sandy while I go back inside to get my car keys?"

My feeling of being sorry for myself subsided somewhat when we reached the dog park. Sandy and Tiny both loved the dog park, with all the interesting smells of the kangaroos and rabbits.

Lately, I had been in the habit of keeping Sandy on her leash, even though it was a council-designated off-leash area, as we had both been threatened by an off-leash pig dog only weeks earlier. While I thought neither of us looked like wild pigs, this dog obviously had thought we looked like prey, and I'd had some scary moments before the dog's owner managed to get control over the dog and drag him away. I was lucky that Sandy had been on her leash at the time. I had reported the incident, and found that there was a Dangerous Dog Order on the dog, and that the owner had disregarded it by allowing the dog off her property. Dogs are not the actual problem—it's their owners, but nevertheless, there was no way I was letting Sandy off-leash in a public place again.

I was so lost in thought that I didn't see that Mr Buttons had let Tiny off his leash. "Oh no, Mr Buttons," I exclaimed. "Keep him on the leash! It's not safe."

"What could possibly happen?" Mr Buttons said. "He's a well behaved dog. He won't run off."

I simply shrugged, and huddled into my scarf. I had a sense of foreboding, but no clue as to why. We hadn't walked far when I saw a red toy poodle approach, along with the person of Cynthia Devonshire. I had not groomed this poodle. It had a show clip, but I didn't want Cynthia as a client at any rate.

When we drew closer to each other, she stopped, and looked down her nose at us. "I do hope your dog is a girl," she said, in a snooty tone.

"Yes, she is. Why?" I asked her.

"It's Gigi's *time*," she said in a lowered tone, while looking around the grounds furtively.

"Her time?" I said, followed by, "Oh. Well, she shouldn't be out in public, surely."

Cynthia shrugged. "She's a small dog. I can easily pick her up if any male dogs approach. Gigi loves her walks, and I thought it was cruel to keep her locked up. I've been coming here at this time for days, and I haven't seen a single other dog at all. Just as well, as Gigi is an Australian Champion show poodle. It's very hard for the reds to do well, you know. Her real name is Floudles Princess Gigi Auburn Luxe. Floudles is my registered kennel name."

"What a lovely name," I lied, but was prevented from saying more by an ear-splitting scream. I looked down at my feet to see Cynthia lying face down on the dirt, her fingers trying hard to hang onto the last vestiges of Gigi's leash as it slipped through her French-polished fingertips.

Tiny had appeared on the edge of the gully, and clearly, Gigi found him highly attractive. Gigi took off towards the edge of the gully, and both dogs disappeared out of sight.

"Watch them!" Cynthia screamed at Mr Buttons.

"You want me to watch them?" Mr Buttons asked. I had no idea why he was so puzzled, but after Cynthia screamed even more loudly, "Yes, watch them!" Mr Buttons hurried into the gully.

I tried to help Cynthia to her feet, but abandoned that idea after she called me a few words that would even make my cockatoo blush.

So I stood there, waiting for Mr Buttons to

THE PRAWN IDENTITY

capture Tiny and return, trying not to watch Cynthia as she climbed to her feet. I knew that Tiny had not been neutered yet, as he had a little abnormality and was on medication. Once that worked, he could be neutered. I hoped Mr Buttons caught Tiny before the inevitable happened, but judging by the sound of rustling bushes at the bottom of the gully, I figured that the inevitable was already in process.

After what seemed an age, Mr Buttons appeared, with Gigi in his arms and Tiny on the leash.

Cynthia snatched Gigi from Mr Buttons' arms. "What happened?" she screamed.

"Yes, I can confirm," Mr Buttons said, nodding his head.

I was puzzled, and was about to ask what he meant, but Cynthia beat me to it. "What do you mean? Confirm?" she bellowed, clutching her little dog to her chest.

It was Mr Buttons' turn to look confused. "You told me to watch," he said. "I thought that was strange, but I did as you asked. I did watch, and so I can confirm that Gigi and Tiny will be parents in the coming months."

Cynthia's complexion turned from white, to

green, to purple-red, all within seconds. She then let out a stream of expletives, and finished by screaming words which included *sue* and *lawyers*, before storming off.

"She's a strange one," Mr Buttons muttered, scratching his head.

I just stood there. What could I say?

The heavy presence still hung in the air when I dropped off Mr Buttons and Tiny at the boarding house and continued down to my cottage. It was with a sense of dread that I let Sandy into the back yard after her morning walk and headed back up to the boarding house. I waved to Greg, who was just setting out on his daily walk.

I walked inside to see a busy Cressida running around this way and that, clutching papers in her hand.

"Morning," I said.

Cressida looked up at me for a moment, but her eyes fell back to her notepad. She scribbled furiously, before looking back at me and smiling. "I'm sorry. I'm just trying to make sure everything is just perfect so that horrible Franklin Greer will have no excuse for shutting the place down. It's so stressful," she groaned.

"Look on the bright side," I said, in an attempt to cheer her up. "No annoying guests to deal with other than Greg."

Cressida put her papers and pen on a nearby burr walnut credenza, and rubbed her temples. "There's just so much work that goes into preparing for a huge inspection like this. They could find any stupid little thing. Even something as small as a faulty wire could shut us down for months, and cost tons in renovations and repairs. I just want it to go smoothly and have nothing else crazy happen. At least for a few days!" Cressida took a deep gulp of air before sinking into the nearby worn Victorian grandmother chair. Its upholstery had seen better days, but that was the least of Cressida's worries.

I leant against the credenza, careful to avoid the fortune's worth of Mary Gregory ruby glass that adorned every available space. "It'll all work out. We'll be fine in the end," I said lamely.

Just then, I heard Mr Buttons' voice outside. Another voice joined his. It sounded more like painful moans than conversation. The door flew open to reveal Mr Buttons helping a dirty, dishevelled Greg into the boarding house.

"Someone almost killed me!" Greg yelled. He

separated himself from Mr Buttons and stepped forward, limping badly. "I'm not sure who it was, but I saw the make and model of the car, and got most of the license plate. I'm a number off, but I think that should be enough for the police. I just couldn't tell if the last digit was a three or an eight. It all happened so fast." He took a deep breath and wiped some dirt from his face.

Cressida and I looked at each other before both turning towards Mr Buttons. The three of us traded glances, clearly trying to tell each other how shocked we were without uttering a single word. "Are you hurt?" Cressida asked him, clearly concerned.

"Yes, of course I'm hurt," Greg snapped. "I just told you that someone tried to kill me!" He was hunched over in a semi-standing position with his hands on his knees. After a few quiet moments, he stood slowly before speaking again. "It was a dark blue Honda Civic. It looked like a newer model, and I got most of the license plate, but not all of it. I was lucky to see it at all. The car drove straight for me! I only avoided the thing because I jumped out of the way at the very last second."

"Greg, sit down, dear," Cressida said, as she walked closer to him. She gently gripped his hand and led him to the grandmother chair on which she had been sitting. "We'll get Blake down here so you can file a report."

"I'll call Blake right now," I said, pulling out my phone. I stepped away from the others, as the phone continued to ring.

"Hello, Sergeant Blake Wessley."

"Hi," I said, feeling my cheeks turn red. "I was just calling to let you know that we have a situation. Looks like another crazy thing happened already."

"Excuse me?" he said, clearly confused.

"Greg just went out for a walk and someone tried to run him over," I blurted out.

"Really? Well, I'll head down there now to take a report."

"Thanks, Blake." I ended the call and rejoined the group.

Greg was still talking about the incident as I approached. "I swear, they were trying to take me out, whoever it was. Maniac!" His voice rose in volume. "First they tried to make it look like a simple accident, but since that backfired and hit the wrong target, the murderer's going all out to get the job done. This is ridiculous! Those tree hugging hipsters need to be run out of this town!" He waved his hands in the air dramatically.

"I just got off the phone with Blake, and he's on his way," I said. "Greg, shouldn't we call an ambulance or take you to the hospital?"

Greg shook his head. "Thank you, but no," he said. "I'll be fine. I'm just stiff and sore."

I watched Greg as Cressida fussed over him, trying in vain to make him agree to go to the hospital. He was covered with dirt and had several rips and tears in his clothing. There was a black mark on his face, but I couldn't tell if it was a bruise or simply dirt.

When Blake arrived, Greg once again went into detail about his near miss, and how he manoeuvred out of the way just in time to avoid being hit, and thus either killed or seriously wounded. "I think there's a strong chance the same person just tried to kill me a second time," Greg said, through clenched teeth.

Blake nodded, and then turned to Cressida. "So, I heard there was another issue here recently also. Something about the victim's missing shoes?"

"Oh, yes. It was just a big misunderstanding, but we sorted it all out. We have the shoes bagged in that brown container right there," Cressida said calmly, pointing to a bag at the front door.

"Okay, thank you. I'll be taking those into evidence. What can you tell me about them and how they were taken?"

"Our cook, Dorothy, and Lisa had a bit of an argument the night before she died. Greg noticed that Lisa's shoes were missing and mentioned it to me, and after a little digging, we found them. Dorothy stole the shoes so she could prank Lisa with some stinky fish or something. When the body was found soon after, Dorothy panicked and cleaned the shoes before returning them to the Lost and Found."

"Is Dorothy here right now?" Blake said. "I'd like to have a word with her, if I may."

"She has the afternoon off, but she'll be back tomorrow."

"Thanks, Cressida," Blake said. "I just have one question that's bothering me. Did the protesters who were boarding here get forced out by the council?"

"Yes," she said.

Blake jotted down some notes in his pad and

looked back up, his face partially obstructed from my view. He leant forward. "I don't know what happened, but I will find out."

CHAPTER 19

*J*eeves was a model client: polite, well-mannered, and easy to talk to. And his owner was a dear as well. Rebecca Williams was the wife of the only lawyer in Little Tatterford. Jed, her husband, had a well-deserved reputation as an ambulance chaser. Cressida had to block his numbers after he habitually called her after every crisis. I could count myself lucky that I'd been fortunate enough not to run into Jed during Jeeves's grooming sessions.

Rebecca, unlike her husband, was quiet and shy. She was sweet and absolutely doted on her bulldog, Jeeves. The dog was like a son to her. Rebecca arranged play dates and baked him organic dog treats from a recipe she had found online. She even paid me extra for a special order of a specific brand of shampoo, meant for humans, for Jeeves's grooming sessions. The shampoo I had in stock was in fact better, but I had found out long ago that many animal owners preferred their own unsubstantiated beliefs to proven facts.

Rebecca liked to chat while I groomed Jeeves, and I always allowed her to do so. It was difficult to groom long haired dogs when owners wanted to stay and talk, but as Jeeves was short haired, his regular treatment was simply a shampoo, condition, and toe nail clip.

"Jeeves looks so happy," Rebecca said, as she offered me a glass. "I hope you like strawberry lemonade. I found an all-natural recipe I was dying to try out."

"Thanks," I said, as I accepted the glass and took a small sip before setting it down to finish brushing Jeeves. Rebecca was handy with home made things, although I always thought that she might be trying a little too hard to impress. I imagined it got lonely in her big house while her husband was working long hours. "How have things been?" I asked her.

"Great!" Rebecca said quickly, although she gave a wistful sigh. "I just hope that Jed remembers to take time off for our anniversary next week. He's always so busy. I really don't know how he keeps up with it all. It makes my head swim."

"I can imagine," I said with sympathy. "I'm sure he has a dozen reminders around everywhere to take a break for your anniversary."

"I'm sure you're right." Rebecca chewed on her bottom lip and then gave a dry laugh. "Ah well, just as long as the whole thing with that land development deal doesn't give him any wild ideas. That man is going to make millions off his wife's death."

"Greg?" I gasped and nearly dropped the expensive bottle of shampoo. I swung around to look at Rebecca in surprise. The woman blinked and gasped as her mind caught up with her chatter.

"Oh, don't pay me any mind. I shouldn't be saying anything about that." Rebecca waved her hand in a nervous flurry.

"But how is Greg going to make millions off his wife's death?" I asked in confusion.

Rebecca stared at me in fright. "I don't know any details, Sibyl." She made a half laughing, half choking sound. "Please, Sibyl, please, please don't mention anything about it. Everything clients tell my husband is supposed to be confidential. Jed would be furious if he found out that I blabbed. You're just so easy to talk to and, and, well, I..." Her voice trailed away.

I nodded at Rebecca in reassurance. "I understand. It's all right."

"Thank you, Sibyl."

Jeeves whined and fidgeted in the tub, apparently picking up on his owner's distress.

Rebecca refused to give any further details, but it was clear to me that there was a lot more to the slip. I tried to piece it together as I finished grooming Jeeves. Why would Greg make millions from his wife's death? Insurance? That was beyond my comprehension. Even if his wife carried that kind of policy, why would Greg be talking to a small town lawyer about it? Why not his own? I imagined Greg had a whole team of lawyers. Why Jed?

Whatever was going on, Rebecca had been dying to say something to somebody about it. It sounded like more than an insurance matter to me. But what?

After I'd finished grooming Jeeves and had left the property, I pulled out my phone and called Blake's mobile phone. To my relief he picked up on the second ring.

"Hey, Sibyl."

"Hi." I felt sick to my stomach. Perhaps it was simply my imagination, but he had sounded a little annoyed that I had called. "Sorry if I caught you at a bad time, but have you heard that Greg would make millions from his wife's death?"

"Say what?" Blake asked in a distracted tone.

"I heard around town that Greg stands to make millions from his wife's death. Is that possible?"

"Sibyl, I'm sorry." Blake cut me off. "I'll call you back shortly. Something's come up."

"Oh, oh, right, sorry," I stammered as I felt my face burn. "Sorry I bothered you."

"It's no bother. Sorry about this. Talk to you later," Blake said quickly, and the line went silent as he cut the connection.

I swallowed, tasting a sour tang in the back of my throat as the drink Rebecca had made me threatened to come back up. Blake and I hadn't really talked since the incident at the café, and I knew he hadn't been happy to see me there. However, I didn't think he would be annoyed with me. I tried to rationalise the situation. Perhaps I had called him in the middle of a job.

Blake also could have been visiting his ex-girlfriend. I stared at the steering wheel as I clenched and unclenched my hands, trying to calm my thoughts. I blinked my eyes rapidly to clear them, replaying the call over and over again in my mind. Maybe he had just been working, or maybe he found the pretty ex-girlfriend better company?

By the time I got home that night, I was no closer to an answer. I fed Sandy and my cockatoo, Max, and then took a bath. I had intended to have a nice, long bath, but my stomach was churning over Blake, so I soon hopped out.

I'd lost my appetite, so instead of dinner, I made a vegemite and cheese sandwich and gobbled it down. Just as I was about to pour myself a glass of wine, there was a knock at the door. I smiled. A visit from Cressida or Mr Buttons would certainly cheer me up.

It wasn't Cressida or Mr Buttons on the other side of the door. It was Blake, and he was clutching a large bag. "Sorry," Blake said. "I haven't been able to return your call, so thought I should come in person. My phone was accidentally smashed."

"Your phone was accidentally smashed?" I said.

"The accident part is probably a stretch. It's a long story." Blake paused. "Mind if I come in?"

"Oh yes, of course." I stood aside to let him in. "Wine? Or are you on duty?"

Blake gestured to his everyday clothes. "Finished for the day. Yes, please." I handed him a glass of wine, and he continued. "What were you saying about Greg and millions? Sorry, I didn't hear it so well. I was dealing with a miniature apocalypse in the park."

To say I was relieved was somewhat of an understatement. So he wasn't avoiding me after all? Blake had already taken a seat on my sofa, so I sat opposite him, my wine in hand. I took a large gulp and then told Blake everything that Rebecca had told me. "And so there's a chance Greg did have a motive for murdering his wife after all," I concluded, "but then again, Rebecca might've got the whole thing mixed up."

Blake rubbed his chin. "I'll certainly look into it."

"So what happened today? You said your phone was accidentally smashed?"

"Rachel threw it onto the highway while we were arguing in the main street," Blake said, before finishing the last of his wine. His brows furrowed into an annoyed expression.

"Oh." My stomach churned. Why was Blake arguing with his ex-girlfriend?

"Yes," Blake continued. "She's one of the protesters, but, I suspect, not for the right reasons. I'm all for everyone having their different beliefs, but she says that ghosts of deceased people appear and tell her things."

I waved my hand at him. "I do believe in that sort of thing, though," I said.

Blake held up his hands in a gesture of hopelessness. "To be specific, back when we were dating, she told me that my grandfather appeared to her and said he had a cat called Patches. I told her that my grandfather and his parents were all allergic to cats, and none of them ever owned a single cat. She insisted that I was wrong."

I nodded. "I see what you mean. I'm sure some people can hear from ghosts, but I'm just as sure that some people think they can, but can't."

Blake rubbed his forehead. "She took a bunch

of essential oils out to the wilderness and poured them on bushes. I told her that type of thing would harm the environment, but she said that a spirit of a wombat told her to do it."

I shook my head. "I'm beginning to get the picture."

Blake let out an irritated sigh. "She's the type of person who would release budgerigars from their cages, despite the fact that they wouldn't survive in the wild. Next she'll probably try to free the animals from the zoo back at her hometown. Today she told me that she planned to climb a tree in the wilderness area and live in it. She threw my phone onto the highway when I went to call her boyfriend to come and take her back home."

"She has a boyfriend?" I asked in surprise. I didn't know what part of that story surprised me more. The mental image of the girl swinging around branches like a monkey, sweaty and her hair tangled like a feminine Tarzan, did not fit the image of the attractive woman I had seen, nor did the fact she had a boyfriend who apparently went along with this kind of stuff. *A boyfriend who is not Blake*, I thought, as my face broke into a wide smile.

Blake nodded. "Todd used to live here in Little Tatterford too," he explained. "Todd has a lot of patience for Rachel's high maintenance, speak-to-the-ghosts-of-wombats thing. I must say, I wasn't happy when she hijacked my lunch table the other day. I tried to convince her not to cause this place trouble and just go home. I've told her several times this nonsense was affecting people I care about."

I smiled in relief. So that's what all this was about? I wasn't sure I understood the whole thing with ghost wombats and trees and such, but Blake hadn't been trying to avoid me. That much I understood.

I walked over to the kitchen to find something to eat with the wine. A quick look through the cupboards revealed cockatoo food and dog treats, but not much else. My eyes fell on the large bag that Blake had placed on the countertop. "Is that food?" I asked hopefully.

Blake stood up, and walked over to me. "It's for you," he said.

The first thing I saw when I opened the bag was a splash of colour. I blinked in surprise. I reached into the bag and pulled out a lush bouquet of exotic, purple dendrobium orchids surrounded by tropical leaves.

I turned to Blake, who was smiling nervously as he watched my stunned reaction.

"Thanks, Blake. They're gorgeous."

Blake took a step closer to me.

"I was starting to think you were fed up with me."

"What would make you think that?" he demanded, with genuine surprise on his face. There was no faking that expression.

"Well, you're always having to save me from trouble." I touched a delicate petal on the bouquet, blinking away a misty haze that clouded my vision. "And I thought perhaps, well, you've been so irritated lately. Um, I thought that you might have gotten tired of my meddling in the town's unsolved mysteries."

I looked back up, and saw nothing but Blake's eyes staring right into mine. He had leant in so close that I could feel his breath on my cheek. I took a short breath. My heart was beating out of my chest.

"Never," he said softly, as he slowly leant closer. He hesitated, as if giving me a chance to push him away.

I closed my eyes as he pressed his lips against mine. I leant into the kiss as the entire world seemed to light up. Everything melted away into that one moment, until only the feel of his lips on mine remained.

CHAPTER 20

The boarding house had been a ghostly sight of late, with most of the guests gone. I was sitting at the kitchen table with Cressida, who was going over some paperwork, when Mr Buttons served us steaming coffee. "Here you go, ladies," he said, extending the mugs to each of us. "I have lowered my standards and served you coffee instead of tea. I figured you could use some serious caffeine if you're going to spend another day going through all those records and whatnot."

Cressida looked up at him, her eyes slowly transitioning from the papers that were sprawled out across the table, to Mr Buttons' looming presence. "Records and whatnot?" she said. "I'm trying to find proof of every previous inspection we've had done. I know they should have this information somewhere in their systems, but maybe if I can show that awful Franklin Greer proof that we have no history of complaints or failed inspections, he might just close the investigation and let us reopen." She looked away, clearly upset. "If we remain closed too much longer, it could end up being a permanent closure. I'm losing too much income right now, and still incurring most of the normal operating costs."

I frowned and looked into my coffee mug. I swirled my finger around the rim and thought about what it would mean if the boarding house had to close. Mr Buttons and Cressida continued their conversation. I heard their voices, but the words were jumbled and only my own anxiety could be heard clearly. Would I have to move and find a new place to live? Would my close friendships with these people be damaged in any way by such a devastating event?

I came back to the present when I heard Mr Buttons asking about Dorothy again. He was persistent, that was for sure.

"No, I'm sure it isn't Dorothy," Cressida said calmly. She had set her papers aside and was staring at her laptop, her fingers tapping the keys in rapid succession. All of a sudden, she gasped.

"What is it?" I asked, as Mr Buttons and I moved to look over her shoulder.

"Cynthia Greer!" Cressida exclaimed, jabbing one finger at the screen. "I googled Franklin Greer and Little Tatterford, and a link to an old photo of Cynthia Devonshire just came up, under the name Cynthia Greer!"

"Greer," I said. "So the rival B&B owner's maiden name is Greer, just like that horrible council man, Franklin Greer."

Mr Buttons stepped back and gasped. "Does that mean that Franklin Greer from the Little Tatterford and Shire Council is that woman's brother?"

I nodded. "Most likely."

Cressida remained silent for some time. When she finally spoke, her voice sounded frustrated, as well as angry. "So that's why they're making such a big deal about the balcony. They're using that poor woman's death as an excuse to shut us down so they can get an unfair advantage and steal our customers. We need to do something."

I looked at her sympathetically. "If Franklin

Greer is her brother, then the case against the boarding house will be thrown out."

Mr Buttons shook his head. "We don't even know for sure that they're related. Maybe it's just a coincidence that they share the same last name."

"It would be a bit too much of a coincidence," I said, "and it gives us another suspect. A new B&B moves into town; a murder happens at the leading business in the same field, and then the rival business owner has her brother shut down her rival for a building code violation." I shook my head. "Now that I've said it, it actually doesn't sound like a viable motive for murder," I finished lamely.

Cressida nodded. "I have to agree. It's not as if this is a million dollar business or anything. It's a stretch to think that the murder was the catalyst for this entire financial sabotage. However, who's to say that one or both of them weren't involved? Maybe that was part of their plan all along."

I shook my head. "Cynthia and Franklin Greer had no motive for murdering Greg's wife. Everything does fit, except the motive. Why would they single out Greg or his wife if their goal was to disable your business?"

"Maybe there wasn't a specific target, and they just wanted to hurt and not kill someone. That would make sense, if their motive was simply to hurt someone," Mr Buttons said. "But my money is still on the cook."

I rolled my eyes.

"Lord Farringdon says it wasn't Dorothy," Cressida insisted, and right on cue, the fat cat appeared and made loud purring sounds around her legs.

"Why don't you ask Lord Farringdon who the murderer is, then?" I asked. The words were out before I could stop them. I didn't mean to sound sarcastic.

Thankfully, Cressida did not appear to have taken offence. "It doesn't work like that," she explained patiently. "Lord Farringdon is a cat."

I felt the beginnings of a headache, but Cressida pressed on. "I think Greg could still have something to do with it, but it all makes you wonder, that's for sure." Cressida sighed, and went back to sorting through the layers of papers that littered the large table's entire surface.

Mr Buttons and I looked on quietly. After a few minutes of silence and coffee sipping, Greg walked into the kitchen. "Good morning, everyone," he said.

"Morning," we replied in unison.

"How are you this morning?" Cressida asked him.

"I can't help thinking about poor Lisa." Greg turned away and covered most of his face with his hands. Sobs could be heard through his makeshift blindfold. "Bless her soul." His hands fell from his face. "First the balcony, then the vandalism, and then they followed that up by trying to kill me with a car."

Greg wiped away the invisible tears, and then poured himself some coffee. I watched as heat escaped his cup and thought of the steam as the pile of lies that he was letting escape from his mouth. I felt his grief was nothing more than a case of terrible acting. Mr Buttons suspected Dorothy of the murder, and Cressida suspected Greg, but was now also considering Cynthia Devonshire as a suspect, but I just could not evade one nagging sensation. Every time something happened with Greg, the hairs on the back of my neck stood tall.

Just then, the door flew open and Greg's personal assistant, Julie, walked in, taking long strides as she approached her boss. Greg rose to greet her. "Julie, what are you doing here?"

"Oh my gosh! Are you okay?" she said in a way that reminded me of the annoying, popular girls from high school. "It's going all around town that you were almost killed! One of those crazy people tried to run you over? Did they catch him? Is he in prison yet?"

Judging by his reaction, the barrage of frenzied questions had caught Greg completely off guard. "Listen, you need to calm down," Greg said in a soothing, serious tone.

The woman ignored him. "Just tell me what happened," she continued, "and why haven't you even called me to tell me what happened? I thought we were friends, not just colleagues!"

"Julie, you're my employee, and that's as far as anything goes between us," Greg said. His face had turned bright red, and I could see he was having trouble keeping himself under control. "I was going to explain what happened to you once things cooled down and this place opened back up."

"Employee?" she yelled. "How dare you! You've certainly changed your tune!"

I watched with interest—this was almost as

entertaining as an episode of *The Real Housewives of Melbourne*.

The young woman's voice steadily increased in volume, until she was yelling at the top of her lungs. Lord Farringdon let out a loud yowl and ran from the room, his tail fluffed out like a toilet brush. Greg tried to lead Julie out of the kitchen, but she was having none of that. "Please, calm down," he said for the umpteenth time. "Let's go outside and we can talk about this in private."

"In private?" she yelled, pointing to us. "Are you afraid that they might hear something incriminating? Are you worried some of your little secrets might get out and see the light of day?"

Oh boy. I glanced at Cressida, who returned my look of astonishment. Mr Buttons' eyes were glued to the scene unfolding before our eyes.

"Julie, I'm warning you. Keep your mouth shut, right now."

The personal assistant didn't respond, but it was obvious that holding her tongue wasn't an easy feat.

"Let's go upstairs and talk about everything," Greg said, in a now calm voice. He gently put his hand behind Julie and nudged her in the right direction. They had only reached the door when things fell apart again.

"I just don't understand why you didn't call or even message me about it. I was worried about you. I found out from a random person at work that my boss, someone I care about deeply, was nearly killed. I'm just hurt and upset." The young woman's words sounded truthful and full of pain.

Greg did not respond, but guided Julie through the door and shut it.

"You just don't get it," he yelled. By now, they were both out of sight, but their voices were as loud as ever. "You're nothing but an employee, and that was only until someone better came along. You're jeopardising everything, and you need to remove yourself from this."

"What? What does that even mean?" The woman's voice sounded desperate. "What are you saying?"

"It means that you're fired," Greg yelled. "Get out, go! I didn't call or text you about it, because I don't want or need you around me anymore. Please, just go. Find yourself a new job. I'll give you a good reference; you don't need to worry about that."

Suddenly, the young woman's voice erupted,

causing me to flinch at the startling shriek. "You know what? You're nothing but a con artist, a liar, a cheat, and a huge jerk! All of this craziness is happening just because you wanted all of your wife's money, and now you're getting rid of me to cover it up further. This is all insane. Actually no, *you're* insane!"

I could hear her footsteps thumping away from our direction, but the sound was soon interrupted by Greg's loud voice. "Julie, stop this. Just wait. I'm sorry! Wait!"

"No!" her voice yelled back. "You made your decision, and that's fine, but now I'm going to make mine." Her voice faded.

Cressida leant forward and looked over at us. "What money? Greg's wealthy. He has no need of his wife's money."

"Obviously we missed something," I said. I hadn't told Cressida or Mr Buttons about what Rebecca had said, as I had practically promised her to keep it to myself, but it was all starting to add up.

CHAPTER 21

Mr Buttons jumped to his feet and ran out the kitchen door, presumably after Julie. I glanced over at Cressida with bewilderment. With just one look and no words, Cressida was able to convey to me one instruction: *Follow!*

Both of us leaped up and dashed out of the kitchen to the front door. When we got outside, Mr Buttons was already locked in conversation with the woman, and Greg was nowhere to be seen. "I'm sorry. I shouldn't have said anything in there. I was just so upset."

"I understand that, Julie, but I think you need to explain what it meant," Mr Buttons said.

"I need to explain what it meant? What is it?" Julie asked, seemingly confused by the question.

"What you said inside," Cressida added.

"You told Greg that all of this craziness was happening just because he wanted all of his wife's money. Those were your exact words, or something to that effect, I think," I said.

Julie looked at me for a while. After a few minutes of silence, she spoke. "I shouldn't have said that," she said softly. She turned away from the three of us and looked off into the distance. We looked at each other, but nobody as much as whispered a word, until Julie continued. "I don't know if he hurt Lisa, or exactly what he has or hasn't done, but I do know for a fact that he knows more than he's telling everyone else. I've seen his emails; I've seen some of his text messages, and I've heard many of his voicemails. I know more about Greg than his wife probably did." A grim look overtook her features as she let out a loud sigh.

"Then please fill us in," Cressida said, "because ever since Greg checked in, everything has become one big mess. Once everything is cleared up, this business can open back up and avoid closing down for good."

Julie appeared to be considering the matter. "Okay," she continued. "Again, I don't know that he hurt anyone, but I know that he has a motive to have done so. His parents and Lisa's parents are in business together. They've known each other for years, even before Greg and Lisa were born, as far as I know. They offered Greg and Lisa a huge parcel of land right next to the wilderness that Greg's currently developing."

"You're not saying that they offered their kids a big patch of land to marry each other?" Mr Buttons said, in obvious disbelief.

Julie shrugged. "I don't think they saw it that way. They considered it a wedding gift, but the catch was that even after the land was gifted to the couple, Greg and Lisa both had equal say with any development of that land."

"What does that mean?" I asked.

"It means that they both have to agree to it," Cressida said.

"Exactly," Julie added. "In order for anything to be done with the land, both of the owners need to sign a document giving consent."

"I still don't see how that's a problem," I said. "Wouldn't Lisa just consent to developing the land? She'd benefit from it just as much as Greg would."

"The thing is," Julie said, "that parcel of land was wilderness land, too. Lisa did not approve of the development of wilderness land. She was unlike Greg and her parents, as well as his parents. She openly said she would never consent to the development of that parcel of land."

"I take it the land is worth quite a bit?" Mr Buttons inquired.

Julie nodded. "Millions and millions, if it's developed."

"Let me guess," I said. "If one of the owners dies, the other gains total control, right?"

"Yes," Julie said. "If one of them were to die before the other, the land and all of their assets and finances would be inherited by the surviving spouse. Lisa's death means that Greg now owns all of that land as its single proprietor."

Cressida, Mr Buttons, and I looked at each other. Finally! We had uncovered a motive.

"Maybe Dorothy isn't looking like a prime suspect anymore," Mr Buttons admitted sadly. His shoulders drooped.

Julie sighed. "I'm going to head back home.

I've had more than enough of this place, no offence."

We all watched Julie drive away. "I'll have to call Blake and tell him," I said.

"Should we try to stop Greg from leaving until the police show up or something?" Mr Buttons asked.

Cressida shook her head. "No, just stay out of it, Mr Buttons. He's not going anywhere. Where would he go? He's in the middle of nowhere working on a project. He can't just up and leave. He's a well-known businessman. It's not as if he can make a run for it and then hide out in the bush for years like that other fugitive did a few years back."

"Oh yes," Mr Buttons said. "That was Malcolm Naden, wasn't it? He hid out in the bush for seven years, right around these parts. Quite admirable, really."

I shuddered. When driving south, I always stopped for a break at the tiny village of Nowendoc, where Naden had been hiding out prior to his capture. The thought always gave me the creeps.

"It was always about the motive," Mr Buttons added. "Without a motive, I just couldn't let myself believe that a man could be so heartless and ruthless. To murder his own wife for something as trivial as money seems unforgivable in any regard." Mr Buttons looked down at his highly polished shoes.

"Unfortunately, a lot of people in this world are greedy," I said. "It's all about propelling themselves ahead, without any worry or concern for those they had to step on to get where they are."

"True, but some people are much different." Mr Buttons shot a beaming smile at me. "Look at you and Cressida. I couldn't imagine not waking up to her complaining about the business, or her telling me the latest thing that Lord Farringdon has said. Oh, and I can't imagine not having the pleasure of seeing your smile every day. It always makes the day go by just a little faster for some reason." Mr Buttons smiled warmly at me.

I smiled in response. I called Blake to tell him the news, while Mr Buttons and Cressida walked back inside. The phone call was short, and Blake had only said one thing: "I'm on my way. Don't go near him under any circumstances."

I slid the phone back into my jeans pocket and hurried into the house, where I caught up with Cressida and Mr Buttons in the lobby. "Blake's on his way," I said, lowering my voice and pausing before continuing. "Blake said not to go near Greg, no matter what."

Mr Buttons frowned. "But then what do we do if he tries to leave?"

"Nothing," whispered Cressida. "You heard Sibyl. We just act normal, and if he appears to be walking out, one of us will have to distract him or something."

"Distract him?" Mr Buttons and I said together. "But Blake said not to go near him," I added, while at the same time, knowing full well that none of us would pay any attention to that.

"Yes, just talk to him or something. Anything that will keep him here until Blake shows up."

"What are you guys whispering about?" A soft voice broke through the quiet lobby. We broke from our huddle and turned to see Greg coming down the stairs.

"Hey, Greg," Mr Buttons said, in an even tone.

Greg was clutching his laptop as well as a small bag, so I figured he was about to make a run for it. I had no idea where he'd go. I somehow couldn't see him living on witchetty grubs, yams, cicadas, and billy tea out in the bush. Nevertheless, my first instinct was to delay him. "Hey, what was that all about with your personal assistant?"

The inquiry caught Greg off guard. His eyebrows raised and his eyes grew larger. "Um," he stuttered. "What do you mean?"

"Julie said that all of this happened because you wanted your wife's money."

Greg's face reddened, and he looked as if he was choking on something. As I waited for a response, I looked at Cressida and Mr Buttons. They were both standing there with their mouths open, no doubt at me being so bold, or so stupid, as to make such a statement.

Greg finally spoke. "Oh, she's just upset because she wants a relationship with me, and even with Lisa out of the picture, I've made it clear that I'm not interested."

"Okay, that might be why she was upset," I said, "but that doesn't mean what she said while she was upset isn't valid. What money was she talking about?" I already knew the answer, but I wanted to delay Greg.

"I don't know what you're talking about!" Greg exclaimed, his face changing from red to a livid shade of purple. "My wife had money, but I have much more money. I didn't need my wife's money."

I was now inches away from someone I was now sure was a cold blooded killer. "You did need to steal. It wasn't money, not just yet."

Greg's eyes narrowed. "What do you mean?" He lunged at me, but Mr Buttons jumped in between us.

Greg focused his rage on Mr Buttons. "Get out of my way!"

"So you can do what?"

"I just want to talk to her," Greg snapped.

The door swung open. "Oh, well, if you're interested in talking, you're going to love what you're in for," Blake said.

Greg turned around, and at once, his face went a pasty colour when he saw Blake and Constable Andrews. "I didn't do anything."

"That's what they all say," Blake said, as he took Greg by the arm.

"Why the balcony?" Mr Buttons asked.

Greg looked away, but then he smirked. "Why not the balcony? It was a simple matter to call Lisa out onto the balcony. As soon as she leant on it, the railing fell. I'd made sure of that."

"Just tell me one thing," Mr Buttons said. "Did you fake the attempted hit and run?"

Greg didn't offer him the consolation prize of knowing the answer, but he winked at him and smiled once more. He had no time to do anything else, as Blake and Constable Andrews dragged him out the door.

We all followed them out, and Constable Andrews drove off with Greg, while Blake stood next to his own vehicle.

"You got here fast," I said.

Blake nodded. "Constable Andrews was already nearby, but the minute I knew you were in danger, I jumped in my vehicle and floored it. I didn't want anything to happen to you."

I paused, taking in his words.

"Well, I mean any of you," Blake added, looking over at Mr Buttons and Cressida.

"But mainly me, right?" I said.

Blake winked at me.

A car pulling into the driveway interrupted our exchange. A man in a black suit got out and walked over to Cressida. "Are you Ms Upthorpe?"

Cressida nodded.

"I'm Edgar Hughes from the Little Tatterford and Shire Council," he said. "I would like to apologise on behalf of the council. Franklin Greer violated our code of conduct policy by not revealing that his sister was moving her business into town. We've reinstated your health certificates and have cleared you and your establishment to reopen as of now."

"How did you find out that Franklin Greer was Cynthia Devonshire's brother?" Cressida asked him. I could see she was both relieved and angry at the same time.

Edgar looked around briefly before speaking. "Officer Wessley here informed us that Franklin Greer was spearheading an operation to close down his sister's business rival. Upon investigating the facts, we have confirmed that this was indeed the case. Franklin Greer has been fired from the council, and he might be facing criminal charges for tampering."

The man offered his hand to Cressida to shake. "Again, we're very sorry for the loss of business and any other inconveniences that were incurred due to Mr Greer's actions. We will make changes to our policy and procedures to ensure a problem like this will not happen again."

"Thank you," Cressida said.

Edgar Hughes drove away, and we all high-fived each other. "So does this mean that the boarding house is back in business?" beamed Mr Buttons. We all looked at each other and smiled.

"We're open as of right now," Cressida said. Just then the phone rang. She pulled it out of her pocket, and listened for a few moments.

"Are you calling from another number?" she asked. "I have your numbers blocked. No, I not wish to take the Little Tatterford and Shire Council to court for loss of income after Franklin Greer wrongfully shut me down. No, I don't care if you waive your fee in return for fifty percent of the payout. Don't call me again. Goodbye." She hung up and looked at us. "That persistent lawyer, Jed Williams," she said with a sigh.

CHAPTER 22

I sat on the dusty front steps of my porch, a delicate china cup of English Breakfast tea in my hands. Mr Buttons sat next to me, his long legs folded up to his chest. Cressida was fetching herself another tea from inside.

It was evening. The sun was going down, leaving a decided chill to the air, and the three of us all wore jackets. The air was thick with dust; I could almost smell and taste it. I looked out across the dirt path to the eucalyptus trees growing there, and suddenly laughed.

"Good gracious me, what is it?" Mr Buttons asked, looking behind him. "Did Max say something rude? I didn't hear anything."

"Not the cockatoo this time," I said. "How

many times have we done this? A wind-down after a murder mystery."

Mr Buttons made a show of ticking them away on his fingers. "Four I think, right?"

"Five," Cressida said from behind us.

Mr Buttons gasped. "Five? Gosh. That's far too many for one lifetime." He sounded defeated.

"To be honest, Mr Buttons, I think one post-murder wind-down is too many," I said with a laugh. I heard the ting of Cressida's spoon hitting the cup as she stirred her tea before she joined us on the porch steps.

Mr Buttons shot me a frown of disapproval. "I'm afraid I find this all somewhat less funny than you do, Sibyl."

"Oh, I know, I know," I sighed. "It's not the murders that are funny, of course. Far from it. It's just so ridiculous. Do you think we could get movie deals or something?"

Mr Buttons finally smiled. "No, I think the less attention we can bring to the murders, the better. I'm not sure the boarding house needs a reputation quite like that."

"Maybe I should refurbish the boarding house and turn it into a haunted house attraction," Cressida suggested, though it was hard to tell if she was serious. I also didn't think she'd need to refurbish, just hang some more of her paintings around the place.

After shuddering violently, I decided to change the topic of conversation. "A man killed his own new wife just for some money," I said, shaking my head. "They hadn't been married more than a week."

"He never loved her at all," Mr Buttons said quietly.

"I don't know," Cressida said, standing from her chair and moving to the stairs. She stepped down and then squeezed in between us. "I've done some horrible things to people I've loved, though nothing like that, of course."

I thought for a moment. I thought of my ex-husband. He had cheated on me, lied to me about it, and then arranged my murder with the help of his mistress. I used to wonder if he had ever loved me. I wasn't sure of the answer. I never wanted to speak to him again, and even if I did, I didn't really care about the answer to that question. I had moved on.

And then I thought about myself. There had been times, before the divorce, when I had hurt him, hadn't there? Sometimes one hurts someone they love on purpose. Yet starting an argument, saying something mean and biting, was worlds away from murder. I couldn't kill anyone, much less someone with whom I had agreed to spend the rest of my life. Greg had killed Lisa simply to get even more millions. I shook my head at the thought, saddened by what some people would do for money. I wasn't a religious person, but at that moment, I thought that the love of money truly is the root of all evil.

"How is it that you always find yourself in danger, Sibyl?" Cressida asked, raising an eyebrow. "Every time there's a murder—and there have been a lot—you manage to get caught in the middle of them," she continued. Seeing my shocked expression, she spoke again. "Oh, no! I don't mean to sound like I'm accusing you of anything. I mean it! It's just that you need to be more careful."

"But then her knight in shining armour wouldn't be able to rescue her," Mr Buttons teased.

"Oh, come on," I said, feeling myself start to blush. "I just get involved, I guess. If people are willing to kill over such petty things, it shouldn't be a surprise that they try to kill to keep their motives under wraps. They don't have a whole lot to lose, let's face it," I said, sighing again. "Not that I'm happy about it either, mind you. Maybe I should start carrying pepper spray. Or a flamethrower."

"You could just carry Blake around," Cressida said, holding back a laugh. "He seems to do pretty much the same job." Mr Buttons and Cressida laughed in unison, and I felt myself turning more and more red.

"Go &%^* yourselves!" a loud voice sounded out, causing us all to jump.

"Sorry, Sibyl, it was just a..." Cressida began.

"No, that was Max," I interrupted her to explain. Max flew down and squawked loudly in my face, clearly unhappy about something. I excused myself, took him inside and fed him. I thought about trying again to find him a trainer, but figured he'd probably just scare them all off. I considered learning to train him myself, but put that to the back of my mind after Max interrupted my train of thought with a vicious verbal tirade.

I left him on his perch and went back out the front, sitting in the same spot on the steps. The sun, encased by a thick red haze, was lower on the horizon, and the cool air was rapidly getting colder. Leaves dropped off trees and littered the ground as an icy breeze gently pushed against me. I thought that we'd have to move the discussion indoors quite soon, before the temperature became unbearable.

Before I could say anything, I felt something heavy hit my chest, causing me to fall backwards. Sandy was standing on top of me, grinning ear-to-ear and trying to lick my face. I struggled in vain to push her off until Cressida mercifully called her away by offering her a treat. I sat up and wiped my face as Mr Buttons laughed at me.

"Sorry," he said. "It just looked so funny. She's just trying to be sweet." He patted Sandy on the head.

"Well, she's trying too hard," I complained, as Mr Buttons furiously wiped Sandy's slobber off my face with an embroidered handkerchief. "Why can't I have a normal pet? Maybe I should get a goldfish. Surely it wouldn't do anything too annoying." I sighed.

"Sandy's normal enough," Cressida said as she patted an all-too-happy Sandy. "She's just a playful puppy."

"Maybe find out if Blake's allergic to anything

before you go pet shopping," Mr Buttons said with a wink.

"Oh come on now! That's enough," I said, perhaps a little too sternly. "Don't make me teach Max to say something horrible about you."

"I'm not sure Max can say anything more horrible than he already does," Cressida said frankly. "I really think he's reached some kind of expletive limit."

I sighed as Cressida said it, knowing she was probably right. I had no idea what kind of educational limits cockatoos had, and it occurred to me that it wasn't a normal thing to think about.

"I can't help thinking about Dorothy," Mr Buttons said, clearly not trying to hide his disdain. "If only she'd been the murderer."

"Mr Buttons!" Cressida and I exclaimed in unison. "That's an awful thing to say," Cressida continued.

Mr Buttons nodded in agreement, but managed to do so without looking at all sorry about what he'd said. "Yes, all right, I'm sorry," he said in what was clearly a lie. "She just irks me so much. Why you keep that woman employed is a bigger mystery to me than any murder we've solved."

"I'm surprised that Lord Farringdon likes her," I admitted. That cat seemed to be wary of almost everybody, so it surprised me that he'd apparently taken something of a shine to Dorothy. That is, Cressida had. It was sometimes hard to remember that her cat wasn't actually talking to her.

"Well, he's of a mixed opinion on almost everybody," Cressida said light heartedly, as though the cat not really liking anybody was all in good fun. "But despite her questionable cooking, I don't mind Dorothy as much as you two. Besides, hiring good cooks is getting harder and harder, what with all the murders," she admitted sadly. "Not to make myself seem the victim, of course. I'd much rather have problems hiring a cook than being murdered."

"I'll drink to that!" Mr Buttons announced, politely sipping his tea. I considered that he hadn't quite used the phrase correctly, but opted not to mention it.

We sat in the cool afternoon as the sun finished setting, then headed inside and spoke at length. While the murders had no doubt shocked everybody, it was amazing to have friends I knew I could rely on so completely. Time and again we'd been there for each other, and I had no reason to suspect that that would change now. Everything was good and calm again.

"&^%(off, you tramp!" Max yelled loudly. I sighed once more. *Almost* everything.

Mr Buttons stood, stretching his legs. "I want to return home before the sun leaves us entirely."

"Thank goodness we have a home to return to," Cressida said, standing as well. "I don't think you realise how close we were to being shut down permanently."

"I do, my dear," Mr Buttons said. "I don't know what I would do if I didn't see your face any longer and didn't get to taste our dear Dorothy's mediocre food day after day."

Cressida and I laughed, and I rose to hug my friends goodbye. I stood on the dirt path, watching them walk arm and arm back towards the boarding house. When I couldn't see them any longer, I went inside, gathering the cups that had been left behind, along with my own.

My cockatoo began squawking insults as soon as I opened the door, and, after dropping off the mugs by the sink, I rushed to his night cage and threw the blanket over it so he would go to sleep. I went in to rinse out the mugs, leaving them to be washed in the morning. And then I had a long, hot shower.

Afterwards, I climbed into bed and read a book. It was a mystery, a detective trying to track down a killer. I shut the book and put it down. I just couldn't get through it. I knew why.

This was my life now. Danger, murder, mystery. Five times now a killer had come to the boarding house, so close to my home.

The murders were horrible, of course—no one would say otherwise. Yet when the mysteries were unfolding, it was all exciting. I had looked forward to getting to the boarding house each day. I had looked forward to comparing notes and tracking down clues. It was dangerous. I knew that. But it was so much more. It was exciting. I had come to Little Tatterford for a quiet life, to escape my divorce. I had been sad and alone, yet I had gained Mr Buttons, Cressida, and Blake. And as I closed my eyes, listening to the soft hoot of a Tawny Frogmouth Owl that had just awakened nearby and the possums scrambling across my roof, I considered myself blessed that I had something more valuable than money.

The next book in the series is:

Any Given Sundae

***ALL GOOD THINGS* must cone to an end . . .**

Sibyl Potts has finally been awarded her long-awaited property settlement, and the fact her ex-husband has been sentenced for her attempted murder is the cherry on top.

Yet just as all seems sweet in her world, the body of one of Cressida's boarders is found in Sibyl's cottage next to a half eaten ice cream sundae.

Looks like there's a rocky road ahead. When all the evidence points to Sibyl as the culprit, how will she scoop out the evidence and prove her innocence? And will the murderer get their just desserts?

ABOUT MORGANA BEST

USA Today Bestselling author Morgana Best survived a childhood of deadly spiders and venomous snakes in the Australian outback. Morgana Best writes cozy mysteries and enjoys thinking of delightful new ways to murder her victims.

www.morganabest.com

Printed in Great Britain
by Amazon